faded denim

faded denim

color me trapped

melody carlson

TH1NK Books
an imprint of NavPress®

TH1NK Books is an imprint of NavPress. TH1NK is a registered trademark of NavPress. Absence of ® in connection with marks of NavPress or other parties does not indicate an absence of registration of those marks.

ISBN 1-57683-537-5

Cover design by studiogearbox.com
Cover photo by workbook.com
Creative Team: Nicci Jordan, Arvid Wallen, Erin Healy, Darla Hightower, Pat Reinheimer

This is a work of fiction. The characters, incidents, and dialogues are products of the author's imagination and are not to be construed as real. Any resemblance to actual events or persons, living or dead, is entirely coincidental.

Published in association with the literary agency of Sara A. Fortenberry.

Carlson, Melody.
  Faded denim : color me trapped / Melody Carlson.
    p. cm. -- (True colors ; bk. 9)
  Summary: Originally trying to lose only a few pounds,
seventeen-year-old Emily's weight loss spins out of control as she
develops eating disorders until she decides that trusting in God and her
friends can help her regain her health.
  ISBN 1-57683-537-5
  [1. Body image--Fiction. 2. Eating disorders--Fiction. 3. Christian
life--Fiction.] I. Title.
  PZ7.C216637Fad 2006
  [Fic]--dc22
                                    2005036115

Printed in the United States of America

3 4 5 6 7 8 9 10 / 10 09 08 07 06

Other Books by Melody Carlson

Bitter Rose (NavPress)

Blade Silver (NavPress)

Fool's Gold (NavPress)

Burnt Orange (NavPress)

Pitch Black (NavPress)

Torch Red (NavPress)

Deep Green (NavPress)

Dark Blue (NavPress)

DIARY OF A TEENAGE GIRL series (Multnomah)

DEGREES series (Tyndale)

Crystal Lies (WaterBrook)

Finding Alice (WaterBrook)

Three Days (Baker)

one

My best friend is so skinny. I hate her. No, not really. I love her. No, I hate her. The truth is, I think I hate myself. And I hate feeling like this—like I am fat and ugly and like I am a total Loser with a capital *L*. It makes me sick.

But here's what really gets me—the thing that makes me just scratch my head and go *huh?* When did all this happen? When did I fall asleep and get abducted by the body-switchers who did some mean sci-fi number on me and transformed me into this—this *repulsive blob girl*? I mean, I didn't *use* to be like this. Back in middle school, I was superthin. Okay, maybe I was just average thin, but my best friend, Leah, was . . . hmm . . . shall we say somewhat pudgy, slightly overweight, a bit obese, downright chubby.

This is the deal: When I was about thirteen, I had already reached my height, which is about five seven (that is, if I stand extremely straight and stretch my neck until I hear my spinal column popping). Meanwhile, Leah was about four inches shorter and twenty pounds heavier than me. She was a regular little roly-poly back then. But in the past couple of years she got really tall. And now she's like five ten or maybe taller, and she's as skinny as a stick. So sickeningly skinny that clothes look absolutely fantastic on her. And it just makes me wanna pull my hair out and scream! Or just disappear.

Okay, to be fair (to me) I wouldn't feel so miserable about all this if Leah wasn't so obsessed with weight and diet and exercise and health that she's constantly throwing the whole thing in my face, saying stuff like, "Emily, are you sure you want to eat that Snickers bar since it has like five hundred calories that will probably end up sitting right on your thighs?" And when she says things like that it not only makes me want to pig out on the Snickers bar but to go grab a giant-sized bag of Cheetos as well. Like super-size me, please!

But that's not the only problem. I mean, since she got all tall and thin (and did I mention gorgeous?), she's become obsessed with fashion and beauty tricks and the latest styles. Leah studies all the fashion rags (which naturally feature these tall, bony, weird-looking models who really do look a bit like aliens if you ask me — probably a real product of the body-switchers), and she has recently decided that she actually wants to become one of them. At first I thought she was kidding.

"You seriously would want to put yourself in that position?" I asked her, incredulous. "I mean you want perfect strangers gaping at your body while you strut around in some weird and skimpy outfit, possibly with no underwear on?"

"I think it'd be cool." And the mind-boggling part is that she really believes she could make it as a fashion runway model — who, according to her, are the ones who make the megabucks. Although I've also heard that lots of them wind up strung out on drugs, burned out, and just generally messed up.

"That doesn't happen to everyone," she told me. "Those are just the girls who make the news and the tabloids, and then everyone assumes the whole fashion industry is at fault. And that's not fair."

Of course, it doesn't help matters that her aunt is a pretty well-known fashion photographer in New York City, or that she actually thinks Leah may "have what it takes." Although I'm sure aunts are a lot like moms, easily duped into thinking their kids "have what it takes" to do just about anything. Yeah, right.

"Okay, what *does* it take?" I asked Leah several weeks ago. (This was shortly after she convinced me to go on this stupid cabbage-soup diet that was guaranteed to "take off a few pounds" but in reality nearly ended up killing me. I ended up in the john for like an entire afternoon—what a fun diet!)

"What does it take to be a runway model?" She pressed her unfairly full lips together as she considered my question. "Well, it obviously takes some height and, of course, you have to be pretty thin . . . and you need good bone structure, even features . . . and then, of course, you need to have that special something."

"Special something," I said hopefully. Now, I may not look like a runway model, but I am good at making friends and making them laugh. Some people think that's pretty special. Naturally, I don't say this.

"Yeah, kind of like personality. Only more than that. It has to be something that cameras can catch, especially if you're going the print route. Or you need that something extra that shows from the runway—an attitude, you know. You gotta be able to strut your stuff and make people want what you have."

"Right." I nodded as if I understood, but more and more it feels like Leah is speaking a foreign language and I am struggling just to keep up.

"I get to see my portfolio shots on Friday afternoon," she told me a few days ago. "Want to go with me to pick them out?"

"Sure," I offered, having absolutely no idea what I was getting myself into.

So here we are at this fancy-schmancy modeling agency where

all the girls are tall, thin, and fabulous, and I feel like a creature from another planet—the planet where the body-switchers dwell. Uranus, perhaps.

"Ooh," gushes Becca (a Scandinavian-looking blonde). She seems to know Leah and has just joined us to look at the photos. "That's totally scrumptious, Leah." Becca is pointing a perfectly sculpted nail to a shot of Leah, which in my opinion is exposing way too much cleavage, but naturally I don't mention this. I just stand there where these glossy photos are spread all over a counter and try to keep up.

Mostly I wish that I could blend in with the aluminum-looking wallpapered walls, which in reality must make me stand out even more in my "fat" jeans (okay, I was bloated today). I also have on this old hoody sweatshirt that is baggy enough to cover a multitude of sins, although I'm sure it simply makes me look like a cow. I try to shrink away from these two girls, seriously wishing I could just vanish.

"Is there, uh, a restroom around?" I ask meekly.

"Yeah," Leah jerks her thumb to the left. "Down that hallway, on the right."

And then I slink away, feeling dumpy and dowdy and just plain pathetic. I consider leaving this plastic place and going home, except that Leah is the one who drove us here and I can't exactly steal her car, although I do know where her spare key is hidden in its little magnetic box under the right fender. But instead of committing grand larceny, I just go into the bathroom and spend enough time there to make someone think I have a serious bowel disorder. I sit in a stall and read a fashion magazine that someone left on the counter. Okay, call me a glutton for punishment.

When I finally glance at my watch, I see it's nearly five o'clock.

I'm hopeful that this place may be closing soon so I can get out of this stupid bathroom and we can go home and I can forget about all this. I emerge from the john and take an inordinate amount of time washing my hands, the whole while staring at my pitifully disappointing reflection.

These are what I would call very unforgiving lights — a garishly bright strip right above the enormous mirror. I'm sure it's been put there so that models can come in here and carefully examine themselves to detect every miniscule flaw (like they have any), and then I'm sure they do their best to address these minor blips before their next big photo shoot. But as I stand here gaping at my lackluster reflection, my dull brown hair (which needs washing), and my boring brown eyes, I suddenly notice a new zit about to erupt on my chin. I want to cry.

"God, why am I so ugly?" I actually mutter out loud, quickly glancing over my shoulder toward the three stalls to see if any feet (which would be shod in the coolest footwear, I'm certain) are present. Thank goodness there are not.

I silently continue my line of questioning. I really was addressing God, not taking his name in vain. I ask my maker what he could've been thinking when he made a loser like me.

Why do I look like this? Why is my nose too long? Why am I short and fat? Why is my hair plain and brown — maybe I should consider highlighting it like Leah suggested. Why am I so boring and blah and mousy looking? Why? Why? Why?

"Hey, Emily," says Leah as she comes in with a big, black folder, which I assume is her portfolio. "I've been looking for you. Are you okay?"

I blink back what threaten to become real tears and force a smile. "Yeah, I'm fine. What's up?"

She looks more closely at me now. "Seriously, are you okay?"

I stand up straighter. "I'm fine."

She nods but still looks concerned. "Becca helped me to pick out the photos, but you were in here so long that I got worried you might be sick or something—"

"Like when you tried to poison me with your cabbage soup?" I try to sound light.

She frowns. "I told you I was sorry, Emily. I never meant for you to get sick. You're the one who said you wanted to take off a few pounds. I think you look fine."

Fine compared to what, I wonder, *a water buffalo?* But instead of saying this, I point to her portfolio. "So, are they really great? Going to launch your big career in New York?"

She laughs. "Not quite. But it's a start. LaMar says that he might have a job for me next weekend." She kind of smirks. "Okay, it's only a Mother's Day fashion show, but hey, it's better than nothing, right?"

I nod. "Yeah. That's great, Leah. Congratulations!"

She drives me home, gushing about how cool the agency is, and then she changes gears and starts telling me about this new cream that Becca was just telling her about that's supposed to make your thighs thinner.

"Hey, maybe you should try it!" she says, turning and looking at me as if I might be some kind of science experiment for her and her new model pals.

"Try what?" I say, pretending that I wasn't really listening. I had been partially daydreaming—or maybe I just want to appear slightly brain dead when it comes to all her mind-numbing beauty talk.

"That thigh cream." Then she goes on to tell me what it's called and how you have to get it online and on and on and on.

I am so thankful when she gets to my house. "Thanks," I tell her, wondering what exactly I'm thanking her for. The ride or the torture?

"Oh, wait," she says suddenly. "I almost forgot to tell you something." Now she has this mysterious expression on her face, like she's got some big secret. Despite my wanting to escape her, I am pulled in.

"What?"

"In all the excitement of getting my photos this afternoon, I almost forgot to tell you about Brett McEwen."

"What about Brett McEwen?"

"He asked me to prom!" She shrieks loudly enough that everyone in my neighborhood has probably heard her.

"No way!" The truth is, this really is shocking news. I mean, Brett McEwen is a pretty cool guy. And not only is he cool, he's fairly nice too. But he's never really given Leah (or me) a real second look before. Sure, he says hey to us and even chats with us now and then (which I assume he feels compelled to do since we all go to the same youth group), but asking Leah to prom? Well, this is mind-blowing.

She nods, grinning and exposing her perfectly straight teeth, which she got whitened right after the braces came off last fall. "Way!"

"Wow." I just shake my head in amazement.

"I am so totally jazzed. I can hardly believe it!"

"Yeah, I can imagine." And the sad thing is that I *can* imagine. I mean, I've imagined myself going out with Brett McEwen, not to prom, since that's too much even for my imagination, but just someplace ordinary. He's been my secret (like really, really secret—even-Leah-doesn't-know-it secret) crush since freshman year. He leads worship in our youth group and I'm sure, being totally honest here, he's one of the reasons I keep going back. Maybe even one of the reasons that I got into playing guitar.

"At first I actually thought he was teasing me," she's telling me now. "I said, 'Okay, Brett, don't be stringing me along here. I know that you can't be serious.'"

"But he was?"

"Yes! He said that he'd been thinking about asking me out for a few months now, but that he couldn't get up the nerve." She shrieks again. "*The nerve!* Can you believe that? Like he was intimidated by *me?*"

"Well, you are trying to become a supermodel, Leah. Maybe the word's getting around that you're hot."

She laughs so loudly that her classic snort comes out. "Yeah, right. Last year's nerd girl finally thinks she's got it together."

"You weren't exactly last year's nerd girl," I protest.

"No, just brace-faced, kinky-haired, gangly, big-footed Leah Clark. Not exactly Jessica Simpson if you know what I mean."

"Well, the ugly ducking has turned into a swan," I say, trying to sound more positive than I feel.

Her smile grows even bigger. "Sometimes I can't even believe it myself, Emily. It's like I look in the mirror and I have to pinch myself."

"I'll bet."

"Not that I'm perfect." I lean half in and half out of her Honda, and my back is starting to ache from this frozen position. "I mean, especially after looking at some of those photos today." She makes a face. "Some of them were really awful. But like Becca said, it's a good way to see the things that need to be addressed."

"Addressed?"

"Yeah." She nods with enthusiasm. "You know, like with the right makeup or airbrushing and maybe even a little surgery, little nip and tuck, you know."

"Like I'm sure, Leah. Why on earth would *you* ever consider surgery?"

"Hey, I'm thinking about it. But I have to talk to Aunt Cassie first."

"What could you possibly need surgery for?" I ask.

"A breast reduction. Duh."

I blink and then look at her chest. "But why?"

"Because they're too big, silly."

"They're not *that* big, Leah. What are you? Like a B cup?"

She laughs. "I wish. No, I'm actually a C. Can you believe it? I mean like last year I could barely fill a double A. And it's not like I've put on any weight either. In fact I weigh less now than I did as a sophomore. Grandma Morris says it's genetics, from her side of the family. I guess my mom had a set of big girls too. Not that I can remember that . . ." Leah sighs.

Her mom died when she was six. I can barely remember her myself. But I can't help but wonder what her mother would think of her daughter wanting to get breast-reduction surgery when she's only seventeen. I know my mom would totally freak. But then she didn't even want me to get my ears pierced. Fortunately, I talked her into it, but not until I turned sixteen. Talk about old-fashioned!

"Well, let me know what your aunt says," I say, standing up now. "And if you want my opinion, I say don't do it."

She laughs. "Yeah, big surprise there, Em."

"Seriously," I tell her. "I've seen models who've gotten implants just so that they can be as big as you. Why would you want to go the other direction? I mean, you look great, Leah." Then I laugh.

"If you don't believe me, maybe you should ask Brett. I'm sure he'd have an opinion."

Now she gets a serious look. "Do *not* tell anyone about this conversation," she warns me. "Besides, if I do it, it won't be until summer. And I don't want anyone to know. Okay?"

I dramatically press a forefinger to my lips. "Mum's the word."

"Thanks."

"But just for the record, Leah, I think your boobs are perfectly fine!" Then I slam the door and head up to my house. *Breast-reduction surgery!* Get real.

Okay, as I open the front door I am starting to feel angry. Really, really angry. I'm not sure whether I'm angry at Leah for being so skinny and gorgeous and having a prom date with Brett, or just angry at myself for not. Or maybe I'm angry at God for making me like this in the first place. But as I stomp up the stairs to my room I seriously feel like breaking something!

two

I'VE BEEN SAVED FOR ABOUT FIVE YEARS NOW, LONG ENOUGH TO HAVE LEARNED a thing or two about being a Christian. For instance, I know that God cares more about the condition of my heart than the way I look on the outside. But I also know that I am *not* God. And I find it impossible to pretend that I don't care about, or that I'm even okay with, my physical appearance. More than ever, I totally hate how I look.

"Focus on your strengths," I just read in one of my mom's old-lady magazines, "whether it's your hair or legs or eye color or even your toenails. Discover where your beauty strengths lie and start there." Yeah, right. The title of this ridiculous article was "Feeling Pretty Begins Inside," and I couldn't even force myself to read more than a couple paragraphs. After that, I stood in front of my bedroom mirror and started to take a serious inventory of my appearance. After standing there about an hour, I honestly could not find one single "beauty strength" to focus on. It's like I rate a big fat zero.

But it gets worse. I think all this focus on looks is making me eat more than ever. It's like food has suddenly become some kind of escape route for me. Comfort eating, I think they call it. And let me tell you, this porking out to feel better is getting pretty scary. Last night I consumed a whole bag of Doritos, about thirty-two ounces of Pepsi, and a half carton of Goo Goo Cluster ice cream—and that's just the food I actually remember shoving into my mouth. Who knows what might've slipped in unnoticed? But the truly frightening part is that I already weigh more than I've ever weighed in my entire life, and at this rate I'll be bigger than a whale by summer vacation.

To top it off, I just remembered that Leah and I signed up to work as camp counselors at our church's middle-school camp for two weeks in June, and we've been warned about how girls this age can be extremely brutal—on everyone. Now I'm imagining all those wicked preadolescent girls picking on me and making fun of me and totally humiliating me. Meanwhile, beautiful Leah will be considered the "cool" counselor, not to mention the one who all the other counselor guys will be flirting with, which was one of our original reasons for volunteering (to meet cool Christian guys). Why is life so unfair?

"What are you so glum about?" my mom asks me on Saturday morning as I sit glued to the boob tube, spacing out in front of *SpongeBob SquarePants* as I put away my second bowl of Froot Loops. It's my little brother, Matt's, favorite cereal, so he'll probably be really mad when he discovers there are only a couple of spoonfuls left. But he's at baseball practice right now so I won't think about that.

Mom stands beside me now and actually places her hand on my forehead the way she used to when I was little. "Really, Emily, are you feeling okay? You don't seem like yourself this morning."

I look up at her and am about to complain about how fat I am when I realize that her weight problem is even worse than mine. Of course, she simply laughs about her bulging waistline. She says it's "just middle-age spread," which if you ask me sounds totally gross, but she seems to feel that being "pleasantly plump," as my dad some-times calls it, is no big deal. However, Dad doesn't treat my weight gain quite so casually. "Putting on some weight, Emily?" he says to me at least once a week. Or in a forced cheerful tone he'll say, "Hey, Em, want to take a walk with me? We should get some exercise." Yeah, right. Or my personal favorite, "You sure you really want to eat *that*?" And then, of course, there's *the look*—the way his brow creases when he sees me eating something he considers "fattening," or even if he catches me just sitting on the couch. It's like he's really obsessed with my weight lately. Like it's becoming his own personal problem. And I'm thinking, *this is* my *body*—*get over it, Dad!* Of course, I don't say that. I'd rather pretend that everything's cool—that Dad and I are still good buddies and he likes me just the way I am.

"I'm fine," I finally mutter to my hovering mom as I shovel the last soggy bite of sweet cereal in, realizing with some dismay that I still feel hungry. What *is* wrong with me?

"Can you pick Matt up at noon?" she asks as she heads for the kitchen. "I promised to meet Karen for lunch today."

"What about Dad?" I protest as I follow her into the kitchen. "Why can't he pick him up?"

"He's golfing."

I make another groan, for sympathy's sake, and then agree.

"Thanks, sweetie."

"Yeah," I say in a flat voice as I rinse my bowl and put it in the dishwasher. "It's not like I have a life anyway."

"Oh, honey," she says, her voice full of sympathy. "Of course you have a life. What do you mean by that?"

"I don't know . . ."

Then she magically produces a box of Krispy Kremes that I didn't even know were in the house. "Want one?"

"Where'd these come from?" I ask as I take one.

She grins with mischief as she pours some cream into her cup of coffee. "I hide them."

19

I consider this as I take a bite, wondering who she hides them from. But maybe I don't want to know. Maybe I don't even care. The pastry tastes so sweet and rich right now . . . so comforting, distracting . . . that I'm thinking maybe it really doesn't matter. I mean, who really cares how much I weigh or what I look like? It's not like I'll be going to prom or anything. This fact is driven home when, just as I swallow the last bite, Leah calls and begs me to go prom-dress shopping with her.

"I really *need* you," she pleads after I make up an excuse to avoid what will surely be pure torture. "If you don't come with me, Kellie will insist on coming, and you know that would be a fate worse than death. Pleeease, Emily, you have to do this for me."

I consider the prospect of Leah's dad's girlfriend at the mall with Leah. Kellie is one of those women who's in her forties but dresses like she's still fifteen. Honestly, Leah and I are both certain that Kellie believes Britney Spears is still the hottest thing out there. For Leah's dad's sake, we try to humor this woman.

"Okay," I finally say, "but I have to pick up Matt from practice first."

"Why don't I pick him up for you?" she offers. "It's on my way to your house anyway. Then we can leave even sooner."

I agree to this plan, realizing I better start getting ready for our shopping expedition now. I can be sure that Leah will look totally chic, but the mere idea of following Leah around as she tries on size 3 or smaller gowns is so disturbing that all I can do is sit on my bed and stare into space and think about food. Life gets no better when I discover I can't even fasten the button on the waist of my biggest jeans — and they are a size 17, the largest size you can buy in the junior section. After that, it's old-lady clothes that are buried in some "fat-girl" section in the back of the store. Probably right next to sporting goods. I try on a couple other pairs of pants with even worse results, and I finally opt for good old stretchy sweats. Okay, they're a little warm for May, but they'll have to do. I tell myself that it doesn't matter. Nothing matters. I wish I were someone else.

"Hey, you!" calls Leah from downstairs. "Ready to go, Emily?"

"Coming," I call back with fake enthusiasm. When I see Leah, she looks very cool in this great little T-shirt that's probably like a size 0, and a pair of low-rise cargo shorts that show off her thin bronzed midriff and skinny thighs. She's been doing the tanning beds this spring, although I can't believe her dad actually signed for her, but then she can pretty much wrap him around her little finger.

"Sweats?" she says, frowning up at me as I come thudding down the stairs like a baby elephant. "Won't you be sweltering?"

"Nah," I tell her, "I'm fine."

"Fine and *fat*," says Matt as he dashes past me up the stairs.

I take a swing at his backside but miss.

"And *slow* too," he shoots at me as he jumps to the landing and makes a face at me.

"And you're a little brat," I yell up at him. "And your feet stink!" I almost tell him that I ate all his Fruit Loops, but that would probably sound bad in front of Leah.

Leah just laughs. "Come on, Em. Don't sink to his level."

"Thirteen-year-old boys should be locked up until they're old enough to vote or leave home," I complain as we go out the door.

Leah chats happily as she drives us to the mall. I just sit there and listen, barely bothering to nod or say uh-huh when it's socially appropriate.

"What's wrong with you, Em?" she finally asks as she's cruising the parking lot in search of a space.

I consider saying "nothing" but then remember that this is Leah, my *best* friend. Okay, admittedly, she's gotten a little shallow lately. And I know that's just because of her amazing transformation. But she used to be really understanding and supportive. She used to be the one I could tell anything. And if I can't tell Leah why I'm so bummed, then who else is there? Well, besides God, that is, and I'm not sure that's such a great idea—criticizing my maker for doing such a lousy job on me. I really know better than to do that.

"Come on," she urges. "Tell me what's up, Em. Did I do something to offend you?"

"No." I look away, pretending to be searching for a parking space.

"Are you still stewing over Matt's infantile comments?"

I shake my head. "No, of course not! He's just stupid."

"Then what is it?" She waits for a car to pull out, then darts into the vacated space, turns off the engine, and looks at me. "Seriously, Em, why are you so gloomy?"

I turn and face her now, seeing once again how gorgeous she is, how together she looks—even her nails are perfect—and I suddenly feel hot tears burning behind my eyelids. *"I am fat!"* I explode.

Leah looks a little shocked, or maybe it's just that she doesn't know what to say or how to respond to my statement of obvious truth. But she just sits there looking at me as if seeing me for the first time, and this is not helping my problem—not one little bit.

"I—I can't stand myself," I blurt out. "I'm fat and ugly and pathetic and—"

"No, *you're not!*"

"I am!" I say, almost choking on my words, "I am a—a loser, a big fat hopeless pathetic fat-chick loser." And then I lean over and begin to cry—really hard.

I feel Leah's hand on my shoulder, gently patting me, and I hear her saying things, quiet things, like that I'm not a loser, and that I'm really nice and how everyone really likes me and how I'm a good singer and that I play the guitar really well, and just a bunch of really sweet things like that. But that just makes me cry even harder.

"You're the coolest person I know, Em," she says gently. "I love you just the way you are. And you're pretty too. You know that I've always thought that."

I finally stop crying and just look at her. "*I am fat*, Leah." I say it again, maybe just so that I can hear myself saying it. "And I've been eating like a pig, and at this rate I'm going to get fatter and fatter—and I'll end up looking like . . ." I feel tears coming again.

"You're being way too hard on yourself," she says softly.

"No," I shake my head. "I am just facing the truth. And, just like they say, the truth hurts."

She takes in a deep breath and her face gets very serious. This is her I-am-thinking-very-hard expression. And then she quietly says, "If you're really this bummed about your weight . . . then why don't you do something about it, Em?"

I frown at her. "Like what?"

"Like take off some weight."

I roll my eyes at her. "Easy for you to say."

"Hey," she uses a warning voice. "Don't act like I don't know how you feel. Who used to get called Two-Ton Tubby all the time?"

"I never called you that."

"I know." She smiles. "My point is that I do know what it feels like to be fat. And I work hard at keeping it off."

"You really have to work at it?" Now for some reason this surprises me. I mean, I know Leah's turned into a real health nut, but sometimes I think she just talks like that for my sake. "I thought it was just that you got taller."

23

She laughs. "Yeah, right. Okay, maybe that helped. But you know I started dieting a year ago. And I exercise regularly too."

"Regularly, like every day?" I ask with skepticism.

"Sometimes even more than that."

"How come you didn't include me in your little fitness plan?"

She laughs. "Hey, I've tried to get you to work out with me. But you usually blow me off. You know you do."

"I *hate* exercising."

"Yeah, and you never really needed to. I mean *you* never had to watch your weight . . . before." She makes a funny face, like she wants to say something more but is controlling herself.

"So, you agree with me then? I *am* fat?"

"I agree that you've put on some weight." She barely nods. "But you can take it off, Em. I've been hinting at this for months. You just need to change some bad habits."

"Like eating?"

"Like eating *junk* food. Seriously, if I can do it, you can too." And then she launches, once again, into all the things that I should and should not eat and how much I should exercise, and I don't know whether to take notes or just run. But this time, for a change, I'm actually listening.

"It's really not that difficult, once you establish good, healthy habits."

"I just don't think I really can," I finally admit. I want to add *because I'm so lazy* but think better of it.

"Yes, you can!" she says with conviction. "I know you can, Emily. You're a strong person, and I'll do whatever I can to help you."

Right now the only kind of help I'd like is in locating a good cheeseburger, because I feel absolutely ravenous. Of course, I know better than to admit this, since I'm pretty sure that Leah will not approve of a cheeseburger. Nor will she approve of pizza, which would be my second choice. Pasta maybe? Probably not.

As we walk around the mall, Leah continues to go on about diet and exercise—like she actually thinks this stuff is fun. And when she finally allows us to stop to get drinks, she won't let me get anything other than a large bottle of water, which she actually expects me to consume.

"I don't really like water," I say.

"It's good for you, Em. And it keeps you from feeling hungry too." She guzzles hers as we head toward Nordstrom. "Not only that," she adds between gulps, "it flushes out the impurities in your system, and it's really good for your skin. Really, water is your new best friend."

I'm sure the good-for-your-skin comment is directed to the remainder of the zit that's still highly visible on my chin. Well, whatever. I do my best to chug down the tasteless water, wishing for an ice-cold Pepsi instead—even though she's already informed me that soda is nothing but carbs. "Carbs are the enemy," she says again and again.

"I didn't know you were *this* into health," I admit as we flip through the hangers on a formal-dress rack. "I mean, you've told me a few things, but it's like you really have this fitness stuff down."

"Well, I've done a lot of research. But I didn't think I needed to cram it down your throat." She holds up a gorgeous pastel-blue dress with beadwork. "What about this one?"

I sigh. "It's beautiful." It's also tiny, I'm thinking. Like I seriously doubt that it would fit over just one of my thighs. "Is it even your size?"

She grins. "We'll see."

Before long she's in front of the three-way mirror, twirling around in the dress, and it's plain to see that it fits. "It's perfect," I tell her.

She nods. "Yeah, I think you're right. Can you believe how easy this was?"

"For you, maybe." I stare at my best friend and try to remember how she used to look. It almost blows my mind.

"And it could be for you too, Em. If you take off some weight." She frowns at me now. "And, well, maybe take better care of yourself."

"What do you mean?"

Now her eyes light up and I can tell she's getting an idea. "You know that show, *The Swan*?"

I let out a groan. She knows that I absolutely hate that show. Talk about superficiality.

"I know, I know, it's really shallow—yada-yada blah-blah-blah—but what if we gave you a makeover kind of like that, Em? Wouldn't it be fun?"

I consider this, wondering if it's even possible. "Do you think it would work?"

"What do you think?" she says as she gives another spin. "It's pretty much what I've been doing for myself."

I frown now. "Yeah, it is kinda like you've been secretly transforming yourself, Leah, like some kind of stealth swan. And now you've left me in the dust, or maybe it's the swamp, the place where the rest of the ugly ducklings hang out."

She laughs. "Well, maybe you can understand how I've felt all these years."

"But I never did anything to change my looks. It's just the way I was."

"That's right." She nods firmly. "And just think how that made me feel. You never had to do anything and you always looked great."

"Great?" I give her my best skeptical expression as I study both of us in the huge mirrors. Talk about your opposites!

"I thought you looked great, Em."

"Well, that was then," I say, trying not to choke up again, "and this"—I hold up my hands hopelessly—"is now."

"So, you agree?"

"To a makeover?"

"You could be my swan project."

I cock a finger at her. "No surgery."

She laughs. "Deal."

I shrug. "Why not. What could it hurt?"

"Not a thing."

"Bring it on."

three

"THESE THINGS TAKE TIME," LEAH ASSURES ME AFTER I CALL HER UP TO WHINE and complain on Wednesday evening. It's week one in my "swan project" (or is this more like my swan song?), and so far it is not going well.

"I hate jogging," I tell her as I flop back onto my bed in a big, sweaty heap of suffering. "It gives me a headache and makes my knees hurt. And so far I haven't lost a single pound."

"You probably won't lose any weight for a while," she says in a matter-of-fact voice.

"Why not?" I practically scream into the phone. "I've been starving myself and jogging for four days straight now. Shouldn't that make a difference?" Okay, the truth is, I haven't actually been starving myself. In fact, I've been cheating on my diet, more than I care to admit even to myself.

"Because first of all, you need to build muscle," she explains, "and muscle weighs more than fat. So, even though you haven't lost any weight, you might have lost inches. Are you measuring yourself like I told you?"

"Yeah, right." I roll my eyes and groan as I push the damp hair away from my forehead. "So instead of being a fat chick, I get to be a muscle chick? Why don't I just shoot myself now?"

"Come on, Em, you gotta be patient if you want things to change. And you gotta have self-discipline. Are you drinking your water?"

I glance at my ever-present water bottle, still full, sitting on my dresser. "Yeah, but I still don't like the taste of it."

"Have you tried putting lemons in it like I told you?"

"No . . ."

"Come on, Em, work with me here, will ya?"

"I don't like lemons. They make my teeth itchy."

"Teeth don't itch." She lets out a long sigh, and I can tell that I'm pushing her patience right now. "And lemons are good for cleansing impurities from your system."

"Okay." I give in. "I'll try to get used to lemons."

"Good. Now for my big news."

I brace myself. I mean, she's already got a prom date with Brett, and she's also debuting in her big fashion show this Saturday. What next? Has someone asked her to star in a music video? Or maybe she's signed some multimillion dollar modeling contract. "What news?" I ask meekly.

"Aunt Cassie wants to pay for modeling school for me."

"I thought you already did that."

"No, that was just a weekend deal at LaMar's, Emily. It was a good start, but pretty beginner stuff, small potatoes, you know. This is with the American Fashion Institute, one of the best schools in the country. And they have a special two-week class for teens. It's in Chicago and starts the week after school is out."

"What about camp?"

"No problem. I'll be back the weekend before camp. This is such a great opportunity for me, Em. I'm totally jazzed."

"Sounds cool," I tell her, although I really don't see why she wants to do this, plus I know that I'm going to miss having her to hang with during the first two weeks of summer break.

"It's going to be awesome!"

"So does this mean I get a vacation from the swan project while you're gone?"

"No way! You have to stick with this, Em. The goal is to have you looking great before our senior year starts. And it's going to take all summer and a lot of hard work to achieve that."

"I thought the goal was to get me in shape before camp," I say halfheartedly.

She laughs. "That would take a miracle, Em."

"Well, maybe I'll pray for a miracle then."

"Pray that God will give you more self-discipline," she says.

After I hang up I pray that God will keep me from having a heart attack. Seriously, it's like I can't stop panting and sweating. I must be in worse shape than I realized. I finally decide to take a shower and end up staying in there for about an hour. Then, when I get out, I decide to check for any improvements in my physique. But all I see is flab, flab, flab . . . and these blotchy red spots don't make it look any better. No way am I going for a measuring tape. This is totally hopeless. I distract myself from my failure to transform by playing the guitar. I play until my fingers start to seriously ache. And then I take a nap.

I skip the jogging routine for the next few days. Of course, I don't admit this to Leah. But on Friday I do tell her that I don't think jogging really works for me.

"I think it's hard on my joints," I say, which may actually be true. All that weight pounding the pavement could do serious harm to my knees and ankles.

She considers this. "Maybe you should try yoga. I have an old video that I used to use. I pretty much do the whole thing from memory now."

"Isn't that like some kind of religion?"

"Maybe for some people. But I just try to pray and think about God when I do it."

"I'm not so sure . . ."

"Maybe you should join a fitness club."

"Isn't that expensive?"

"You're sure full of excuses, Em. Maybe you don't really want to do this."

"No," I say quickly. "I do. I guess the truth is, I'm just lazy."

"Well, being lazy will not get rid of fat. Only hard work and careful eating will do it."

"Yeah, yeah. I know."

"Are you coming to the Mother's Day fashion show tomorrow?"

"Sure. And my mom wants to come too. Do you think I can buy an extra ticket at the door?"

"I have an extra one. I considered giving it to Kellie but, well, you know how that is. I'd much rather give it to your mom. Next to Aunt Cassie, who naturally can't come, she's been more like a mother to me than anyone else."

"Well, she'd love it."

"Cool. I'll put your name on it and leave it in front."

The next day, I try to dress nicely to go to the fashion show. I'm fully aware that the clothes being shown are not only extremely expensive but supposedly very chic too. But as Mom and I walk into the fancy restaurant that's situated in a very expensive hotel downtown, it's uncomfortably clear that we're both way out of our league. Fortunately, Mom is oblivious to our lack of fashion sense. She is smiling and still commenting on the beautiful fountain in the lobby, and then she praises the flower arrangements, and she honestly seems totally happy to be here. I, on the other hand, wish

I could disappear—*poof*—good-bye.

My floral print skirt, which I used to think was kind of cute, now seems way too tight and rises too high when I sit down—exposing my pale thunder thighs, which are not the least bit attractive. And I'm sure the blouse I'm wearing looks like I got it at Kmart, although it was actually Target (or Tar-jay as Mom and I call it). But worse than this is my mom's outfit. I thought it looked sort of okay when we were still at home. It's a light-blue dress that she's worn to church and weddings and stuff, and I used to think she looked pretty good in it, but now I can see that it's too tight across the bust, making her look even heavier than she is, and the style is so dated that she looks more like my grandma than my mom. We look like a pair of fat frumps who accidentally stumbled into this high-fashion affair, and I am certain that everyone is staring at us, wondering if we somehow walked into the wrong luncheon. I just want to fade into the floral carpeting.

I feel the heat on my face as Mom and I are led to a table, which is, thankfully, way off to the side and not too far removed from the restroom.

"Isn't this lovely?" Mom gushes as she sits down. "Such a treat."

Of course, this only makes me feel guilty. I mean, seriously, why should I be ashamed of my own mother? Or myself for that matter? We are good and decent people. My mom, a devoted kindergarten teacher, is one of the most beloved teachers at her school. Everyone says so. And I have a few things going for myself as well. Okay, I can't quite think of a single one at the moment. Right now, all I can think of is the fact that I would love to be anywhere but here.

Quit being so shallow and insecure, I tell myself as I force a smile for Mom's sake. "Leah says the fashion show is supposed to be really good."

Mom actually claps her hands now. "Ooh, this is so fun, Emily. I can't wait."

Okay, I'm losing it. "I need to use the restroom," I say.

"Oh, good idea." She nods. "You go now so you won't miss anything later."

I quickly exit, hoping that I can gather the nerve to come back and sit down. It would be pretty pathetic to abandon my mom at a Mother's Day luncheon. On my way to the restroom, I see some of the beautifully dressed models loitering in the hallway. I try not to look their way as I go into the restroom. I don't need any more intimidation. Although I don't need to use the john, I actually go into a stall and close the door. I hope this isn't becoming a habit.

But, in the quiet privacy, I actually bow my head and pray. I ask God to give me strength. I ask him to help me to accept myself—and my mom—and not to be so freaked about being such misfits. After all, I remind myself, wasn't Jesus a bit of a misfit when he came to live on earth? Then I take a deep breath and tell myself to just chill, and that I can get through this.

I'm just about to emerge when I hear someone go into the stall right next to me. The next thing I know she is barfing, and the sound of it makes me almost feel like I could hurl too. I flush the toilet, for effect, and then go out by the sinks where I wash my hands, listening to see if this woman is okay or perhaps needs help. But within seconds, Becca (Leah's model friend) emerges and she looks perfectly fine, not to mention beautiful.

"Are you okay?" I ask, eyeing her with concern.

She smiles into the mirror as she washes her hands and blots a damp paper towel to her lips. "I am now."

"Nerves?" I ask as I dry my hands.

"Something like that." Then she winks at me and pushes open

the door, the sounds of her heels clicking on the tile floor as she exits.

Okay, it makes sense that a model would feel nervous before a fashion show. If it were me, I'd probably go to pieces and have to be scraped up off the floor—like I would ever be in a fashion show to start with. But another thought crosses my mind, and I begin to think that perhaps there is more to this story. Maybe Becca isn't just "naturally thin." Maybe she helps herself out with bulimia. I've heard of bulimics—girls who eat too much and then make themselves throw up—but I've never actually known anyone who did it. Or if I did know a bulimic, I wasn't aware of it.

Of course, I tell myself with a slight sense of superiority, that's probably the secret of all those stick-skinny models. They're either anorexic or bulimic. How else could they keep the weight off?

Back in the restaurant, I wonder how many of these thin and chic-looking guests have the same problem. I almost say something to this effect to my mom but stop myself. It's not exactly polite luncheon conversation.

"Are you okay?" she asks with concern.

"I am now," I say a little smugly, sounding a bit too much like bulimic Becca.

"They already brought our lunch," she says, nodding to the two plates on our table. "There wasn't a choice, everyone is having the same thing."

I look down at the salad on my plate and frown. "I hope there's more than just this."

"Shall we ask God to bless it?" she offers cheerfully. Then we bow our heads and Mom says a little prayer. I consider asking God to not only bless it but to multiply it, then decide against that idea.

As it turns out, the salad is the main part of the luncheon.

Fortunately, there is bread too. I boldly ask our waitress for a second helping, which my mom appreciates, but the waitress gives me a look to suggest that she does not. Or perhaps she is thinking that we two fat chicks do not need another portion of bread and butter. Well, tough.

Then the fashion show begins, and I try to pretend I'm someone else as I watch the models parading by, each one thinner and prettier than the previous. And, of course, Leah looks amazing. She has on a lime-green outfit that looks stunning with her golden tan and gleaming dark hair.

"Oh, my," gushes Mom. "Leah has turned into such a beauty!"

I nod and force a smile.

Afterward, we are served petits fours and tea, which, if you ask me, is a pretty pathetic excuse for dessert. As we are leaving the hotel, I offer to get Mom something at Ben & Jerry's across the street to make up for it.

She grins. "Oh, that would be a nice way to end this afternoon!" Then she turns and winks at me. "Well, as long as we don't tell your dad."

And so we pig out on hot-fudge waffle-cone sundaes. And I tell myself that there is no sin in being fat and happy. Except I don't really feel happy. To be honest, as we're driving home, I feel fat and hopeless. But I don't let on to Mom about this. I don't want to spoil this time for her.

four

THIS FEELS LIKE THE LONGEST WEEK OF MY LIFE, AND IT'S ONLY WEDNESDAY. The thing is, it's prom week and I'm trying to keep up this little act I've created, like I'm all happy and fine with the fact that my best friend is going to the prom (with my secret crush) and I am *not*.

But when I see Leah rushing down the hall toward me with this totally devastated expression, I feel strangely thrilled. Okay, I hope no one has died. But I guess I wouldn't be too sad if Brett dumped her just days before prom. I mean, I'd pretend to be sad, and I'd be totally sympathetic, but inside I'd be doing a little happy dance.

I'm really a rotten person.

"Emily!" she exclaims when we're face-to-face. "The worst thing has happened!"

"What?" I say with what I hope looks like real concern in my eyes.

"It's my dad!"

Okay, now I feel truly horrible. Has something happened to her dad? Oh, how could I be so selfish, so insensitive, so self-centered? "What is it?" I exclaim, grabbing her by the arm. "Is he hurt?"

"No . . . no." She shakes her head. "Nothing like that. It's just that he says I can't go to AFI."

I blink. "Oh."

"I'm devastated, Emily. I have to go."

Now my compassion kicks in. Maybe it's because I'm so relieved that her dad is okay. "Oh, Leah, that's too bad. I know how much you were looking forward to it. Why won't he let you go? I mean, your aunt's paying for it and everything. I'd think he'd want you to go." What I don't mention is how Leah's dad usually gives her whatever she wants, not that she's spoiled exactly. Maybe a little.

"He read some article about some totally lame modeling school where there was a sex scandal, and on top of that some girl got raped, and now's he's certain that will happen to me too."

"You're kidding."

"I wish I was. Dad has totally gone into hyperprotective mode. He's put his foot down and nothing I say seems to change his mind." Now she actually starts to cry. "I wanted this so bad, Em!"

I hug her as she cries. "I'm really sorry, Leah. I know you did. I wish there was something I could do."

"I know it's stupid to react like this," she says as she steps back and wipes the tears from her cheeks, "but I just wanted it so bad."

I shake my head. "Maybe you can do it next year," I suggest. "After you graduate. You'll be eighteen then."

She frowns. "Eighteen is almost over the hill when it comes to modeling."

"Oh."

I try to console her during the rest of the day, but she is so gloomy that it's a challenge. Finally, as she's giving me a ride home, I remind her about prom. "At least you have that to look forward to." Then I make a loud self-sacrificing sigh. "Not all of us are so lucky . . ."

She turns and looks at me. "Oh, I'm sorry, Em. I bet you think I'm really selfish. Are you feeling bad about not going to prom?

You've been so cheerful lately that I figured you really didn't care."

"Maybe I should become an actress." I give her a big smile.

"Yeah. Maybe you should give me lessons." Then she frowns again. "But seriously, I would give up prom to go to AFI."

"You would?"

"In a heartbeat. I mean Brett is cool and stuff. But I don't really know him that well and the thought of going with him makes me kinda nervous. We're doubling with Kyle and Krista, you know. And, well, Krista thinks she's all that. I'm just not sure . . ."

"You'll be fine," I assure her. But suddenly, given this perspective, I think I'm actually feeling relieved *not* to be going to prom. Life's weird.

"Thanks," she says. "And thanks for being there for me today. It helps."

"Well, I'll be praying for you," I tell her. "Maybe God can change your dad's mind if it's really the right thing for you to go." But even as I say this, I doubt it will happen. And, to be honest, I don't think I even want it to happen. Not really.

Later that night, Leah calls. "I have the best news!" she practically shrieks into the phone. "You are not going to believe this."

"Your dad changed his mind?" I ask, hoping that I'm wrong.

"Better."

"You won the lottery?"

"No, silly. Listen to this. I told Aunt Cassie the bad news and she came up with a plan. And then she talked to Dad and he agreed. Can you believe it?"

"What's the plan?" I ask with only mild interest.

"You're coming with me!"

"Huh?" I sink down into the couch and try to take this in.

"Aunt Cassie is sponsoring you to go to AFI with me, Emily!

She's paying your entire way. That way we can room together and take care of each other and—"

"Hold on a minute," I say quickly. "I am *not* model material, Leah. Or have you forgotten that?"

"I told Aunt Cassie that you weren't feeling too good about yourself these days, and I even told her about our little swan project. But she said not to worry. She said the industry has become more open to using larger models, that there are magazines that specialize in big girls."

"Big girls?" I want to scream now.

"Those were her words, Em, not mine. All she meant is that size doesn't have to matter—especially just to go to modeling school. It's not like you're trying to get work or anything."

"As a *big girl*, you mean?"

Leah laughs. "Forget about that. All she meant is that you should go. She thinks it will help you with your self-image. They teach about fashion and makeup and a bunch of other things too. In fact, this whole thing will go perfectly with our swan project. Please, tell me you'll do this with me, Emily. It's the only way my dad will let me go."

"Why don't you ask someone like Becca to go with you?" I suggest, feeling this strange sensation of going under, almost as if I were drowning.

"No way. Besides, my dad said you or no one. He totally trusts you, Emily. He knows your faith is strong and he keeps saying how mature you are."

"Mature?" I repeat meekly, not knowing whether to be flattered or insulted.

"Yes. Dad said the only way I can go is if you agree to go with me. And you have to agree, Emily. You will go, won't you?" Her voice has the most pathetic, pleading sound to it. I almost expect her to remind me of how her mother died, of how close we've been all these years, of how she's sacrificed for me in the past, of how she used to be the "fat" friend but never complained . . . but she is too good a friend to mention any of those things.

"Can I think about it?" I say.

"Of course. And I realize there's your parents to deal with."

"That's right," I say, hopeful again. I mean, I can pretty much predict that they would never agree to let me do something this crazy. Modeling school in Chicago? Yeah, you bet. "I do need to ask them."

"And both Dad and Aunt Cassie can talk to them," Leah assures me. "If they have questions or anything."

"Okay." I feel certain I have my way out now. "I'll get back to you on this as soon as I talk to my parents."

Just as I hang up, my mom comes into the living room. "Talk to your parents about what?" she asks as she sits down in the big leather recliner across from me. It used to be Dad's chair, but more and more I find my mom sitting in it.

So I launch into Leah's plan, making it sound as much like a harebrained scheme as I possibly can. But when I finish, Mom is looking thoughtful, like she's actually considering it.

"What a great opportunity for you, Emily!" she finally exclaims.

"You mean you'd really let me go?" I ask, incredulous. "For two weeks? By ourselves? To go to modeling school?"

"Well, of course, we'd have to look into it carefully. And I'd want to talk to Leah's aunt, although I've always thought that Cassie was a sensible woman, even if she does live in New York. But if everything is on the up and up, well, I think it would be wonderful for

41

you two girls to have this time together. Leah has so blossomed this year. And perhaps this will help you too, Emily. You do seem to lack confidence, but you're such a pretty girl. Maybe the good Lord knows that this is just what you need to round out who you are becoming."

Round out? I stare at her. Does she not see how "rounded out" I actually am? Does she not realize that I will be a total misfit at AFI? The only fat girl with a bunch of stick people?

"Oh, I'm so excited for you," she says happily. "This might be just the thing, Emily." And off she goes to call Leah and get Aunt Cassie's phone number. Great.

Okay, I'll admit that I never even had a chance to pray for Leah's dad to change his mind about AFI—although I had intended to do so—but I do begin to pray now. I pray that God will throw a big old wrench into the works and that my dad will totally put his proverbial foot down, and that my parents will play the tough-love card, deciding that modeling school and two unsupervised weeks in Chicago is definitely not the right thing for their little girl.

But within twenty-four hours, it all seems to be out of my hands. Both my parents have decided that this is a *divine* opportunity for me. And no one seems to care about what I think.

"It's just what you need," my dad says at dinner. I can tell he's thinking about my weight as he watches me take a large helping of mashed potatoes. "It will help you on your way to becoming a lovely young lady, Emily."

My little brother laughs and I narrow my eyes at him, wishing I could punch him, but my parents have a serious no-fighting-at-the-table rule.

"Leah's aunt says that it will be sort of like finishing school," Mom says as she passes me the butter.

"Finishing school?" I echo hopelessly.

"Yeah," says Matt with a devilish look. "They'll probably finish you right off."

And for the first time, I think Matt might actually know what he's talking about.

five

IF I THOUGHT NOT GOING TO PROM WAS BAD, KNOWING THAT I'M GOING TO modeling school is worse. Way worse. I have exactly seventeen days to get my act together. That means Project Swan has just switched to fast-forward. No more cheating on my diet or skipping my exercise routines, and I've been drinking so much water that I'm sure I'll be growing fish scales before long. In fact, I'm thinking of taking up swimming, which means I'll have to put on a swimsuit, and if that's not desperate, nothing is. But at least the weather is nice, which means I might be able to soak up some sun (since my parents still refuse to let me go to a tanning salon), because I've heard that a good tan makes you look at least ten pounds lighter.

Leah keeps reminding me that I can't expect miracles in this short amount of time. But I'm doing everything I can to get myself into some kind of shape before we get on the plane to Chicago. Because I'm tired of being humiliated. And I'm tired of being fat and ugly. I'm also tired of looking like Leah's pathetic friend. In fact, I'm just plain tired.

By the time school is out, just two days before Chicago, I am totally dismayed when I hit the scales. After all my hard work and careful dieting, I have only lost three pounds.

"Three pounds!" exclaims Leah happily. "That's great, Emily!"

"Great?" I frown at her. "I've been starving myself for a month and I've only lost three pounds!"

"A month?" She looks skeptical. "You already admitted that you cheated on the diet during the first week or so."

"Okay, fine. But I have been faithfully doing it for almost three weeks."

"Yeah, and you've lost three pounds." She carefully studies me. "And I'll bet you've lost a lot more in inches. Did you measure yourself like I told you to?"

I make a face at her. "I can only handle so much, okay? It's bad enough weighing in every day. Wrapping a tape measure around my big fat thighs might push me over the edge."

"Too bad." She shakes her finger at me. "Because you'd probably be pleasantly surprised. I can see a difference."

I frown as I stare into my reflection in the full-length mirror. I mean, sure, maybe I can see a little improvement, but for the most part, I look pretty much the same as I did a month ago. "Isn't there anything we can do to help me before we go to Chicago?"

She reaches up and touches my hair. "I wish your mom would let you do something with your hair, Em. I think it would look really great with highlights."

I consider this. I mean, it's like my parents are forcing me to go to modeling school to improve myself. Why wouldn't they want me to improve my hair? And, in all fairness, I haven't actually asked my mom about coloring my hair since last year. Anyway, I'm thinking that maybe it's time to take some things into my own hands.

"Why not?" I say to Leah.

"Huh?" Her perfectly arched brows lift in surprise.

"You know, I think I'm old enough to decide how to wear my own hair."

"Yeah, but . . ."

I shrug. "Where do we go?"

So Leah calls around until we find a place at the mall that can fit me in this afternoon. Fortunately, everyone at my house has gone to Matt's baseball game, so all I do is leave a note.

But once we're at the mall, and I'm going into the beauty salon, I get cold feet. I mean, I don't even get my hair *cut* by professionals. For the past few years I've just worn it long, and my mom trims it occasionally. "I don't know . . ." I whisper to Leah as we wait for my appointment.

"Don't worry," she assures me. "This won't hurt a bit."

"But what if it looks terrible?"

"It won't, Emily. Don't go there."

So I try not to, as a woman named Lynette first trims then "weaves" my hair. I just pretend that this is no big deal, like I do stuff like this all the time. And I try to avoid looking in the mirror, since this just makes me feel like freaking, and I don't want to jump out of this chair and make a run for it with Lynette only halfway finished.

Finally she's done, and although I'm surprised when I look in the mirror—like, who is that blonde chick?—I am also pleased. I reach up and touch my hair, almost expecting it to feel dry or stiff. But it's soft and natural. "Thanks," I tell Lynette. "It looks awesome."

"Oh, wow!" says Leah as I go to the front of the salon to pay the receptionist. "You look really great, Emily."

After that, Leah talks me into going to Nordstrom's makeup counter and trying some new things. "Aunt Cassie says they'll teach us a lot about makeup at AFI, but maybe you should have a few things down, just so you don't, you know, stick out or anything."

I give Leah a sideways glance, wondering if she might be as worried as I am about my appearance. But I keep these thoughts to myself as I surrender myself to Leah and the salesperson for cosmetic experimentation. By the time we leave the mall, I have spent a pretty big chunk of change on my hair and face, and I seriously doubt that it will be worth it.

The plan is for Leah to spend the night. She's going to help me pack—to make sure that I don't make any serious fashion blunders—but as she goes through my closet, I can see that my wardrobe is nothing but one great big mistake. The "discard" pile is growing rapidly. Meanwhile, she hasn't found much to put in my suitcase. Finally, she throws up her hands in surrender.

"How can you stand this?" she demands.

I just shrug.

"I mean, your stuff is either too small, although that could change, or it's out of style, or it looks like a bag lady, or is nearly worn out."

"I guess I haven't been that into clothes lately."

"Duh." She holds up a fairly respectable pair of jeans that I haven't seen in a while. "Do these fit?"

"I don't know."

"Try them."

So I tug them on and I can almost button them. "Close," I say, feeling a tiny bit hopeful. "That's better than the last time I tried."

"Well, that's something." Just the same, she tosses them back into the closet. "Maybe by July. Clothes that are too tight just make you look fat."

"Oh."

It's about midnight by the time she gives up. I gave up hours ago. But I'm surprised to find that she's actually done a fairly good job of selecting clothes. Even if I will be traveling light.

"Thanks," I tell her as I check out my hair in the mirror again.

"And thanks for helping me with my parents tonight."

She laughs. "Hey, that was fun. I've never seen your dad at such a loss for words."

"Yeah, at first I thought he was really going to freak."

"I think he actually liked it, after he got used to it."

"Yeah. Even my mom seemed pretty much okay. Well, other than the fact that I did it behind their backs."

"But at least you apologized to them."

I consider this as we're going to sleep. (Leah insists that we get our "beauty sleep.") It's not that I want to rebel against my parents exactly, and I know the Bible says to obey your parents, but I guess I feel I need to take some control of my own life too. In fact, the more I think about it, the more I realize how much I let my parents control me. My dad makes me feel lousy about my weight gain, and my mom consoles me with food. And I have a strong suspicion that's not a good combination.

But as I ruminate over these things (and now I can hear Leah's even breathing, which tells me she's already fallen asleep) I begin to feel ravenously hungry. And then I feel like I'm going to die if I don't eat something sweet. And it occurs to me how I'll be at AFI on Monday and that I probably won't have the freedom to eat what I like, when I like.

Then I remind myself how good I've been doing by not snacking. I can't believe how many fruits and vegetables I've eaten these past few weeks. And I've exercised, sometimes twice a day. And what has that gotten me? All that work and discipline and I've lost a mere three pounds. At this rate, it'll take me a year to reach my goal. If I don't give up. I'm afraid I'll give up.

Finally, I can't take it anymore. I quietly get up, sneak out into the hallway, make sure that the house is silent, and then slip down the stairs. I go directly to the kitchen, and that's when I totally pig out.

I go for Mom's secret stash, hidden in a basket that's stored in the bottom shelf of the pantry. It's the only "safe" junk food because my mom will never mention that it's missing, and consequently my dad will never find out. I quickly put away most of a box of Mystic Mint cookies, washing them down with two glasses of milk (and not the skim milk that Leah told me to start drinking). Then I'm craving salt, so I go for chips. I polish off a bag of Cool Ranch Doritos, along with a lot of Pepsi. And then I'm about to go for a king-sized Snickers bar, thinking I'm still hungry, but then I realize that my stomach is actually aching. It's like I haven't eaten this much crud in weeks, and it's making me feel sick.

Suddenly I feel worried. What if eating like this after you've been dieting is dangerous? I imagine my stomach, stretched beyond capacity, exploding, or maybe I'll have a heart attack. Now I'm getting seriously scared. I even consider waking up my mom. But then my dad would find out, and probably even Leah. And I just don't think I can take that kind of humiliation. On the other hand, I don't want them to find me dead in the kitchen — "she died from eating junk food" listed as cause of death. I am desperate.

I go to the downstairs bathroom and stare into the toilet, wishing I could barf it all up. The weird thing is, I hate throwing up. I hate the feeling of nausea. And yet here I stand wishing for it. And as I stand here, I hate that I've given into eating all that junk. What was I thinking? I mean, maybe losing three pounds doesn't sound like much, but it was a start, wasn't it? And then I go and eat enough food to put on three pounds. What is wrong with me?

And that's when I do it. I shove my finger in my mouth and actually gag myself. I'm amazed at how easy it is, how quickly it's over with, and how much better I feel for doing it. And then I remember

Becca, that day before the fashion show, how she probably did this same thing, and how I judged her for it. As I wash my face with cold water then look at my image in the mirror, I remember how superior I felt to her that day, how certain I could never become like her.

But then I'm not like her, I tell myself as I turn off the light and tiptoe back upstairs. This was a one-time thing. An emergency effort, really. I mean, I could've actually hurt myself with that stupid eating binge tonight.

When I get back into bed, this unexplainable sense of victory ripples through me—like maybe I just missed a bullet. And that's when I remember this old saying my grandma used to like. She'd give it to me when I was being impatient about something or wanted to do two things at once, sort of have it both ways.

"You can't have your cake and eat it too," she used to say. I didn't really get it then, but I think I do now. And I think maybe she was wrong.

six

I'M FEELING REALLY GOOD ON MONDAY MORNING. TOTALLY JAZZED. AND when I look at my reflection in the mirror, I think I look way better than I did a month ago. First of all, there's my hair, which I think looks fantastic. And I've got this little bit of a tan going on. And I'm thinking Leah is right. I have lost inches, because I do look thinner than before. Even my dad noticed. Well, sort of.

"I think you're losing some of that baby fat, Emily," he told me after church yesterday.

Okay, I would've appreciated a different sort of compliment. I mean, like one that actually felt complimentary. But, hey, it's my dad. I take what I can get, right?

"I have an idea," my mom said then, perhaps as a buffer to my dad's less-than-sensitive comment. "Why don't you and I go shopping this afternoon, Emily? We'll get you something special to wear to Chicago."

So it is that I'm wearing a completely new outfit—some very cool capri pants and a T-shirt that I've topped with this little denim jacket. Okay, the jacket's not exactly "little," but it's cute. And, okay, it's probably not anything as cool as what Leah will be wearing today, but it's definitely an upgrade for me. And I think I look pretty good. And I think I'm ready for AFI. I just hope they're ready for me.

My mom drives us to the airport. Leah suggests that she just drop us at the entrance, since Leah has flown a lot, both with her dad and on her own. She goes to see her aunt at least once a year. But my mom insists on parking and going through check-in with us, and then, even after I assure her that we'll be perfectly fine, she wants to walk us to the security gate.

"Do you girls need something to snack on during the flight?" she asks as she points to a McDonald's. "I've heard that flights don't serve much food anymore."

"It's only a two-hour flight," Leah reminds her.

"But you never know," my mom persists. "You could be delayed."

"We'll be okay," I tell mom.

"And we'll pick up some bottles of water," says Leah. "As soon as we get through security."

Mom frowns. "That's all you want? Just a bottle of water?"

"We'll be fine, Mom," I say to her, pausing to set down my bag and give her a quick hug. "Really. Don't worry. We won't starve before we get to Chicago."

She smiles. "No, no, of course you won't." Then she hugs Leah too. "You girls look so grown up today. It's hard to believe that—" And then she actually begins to cry.

"Oh, Mom!" I say, giving her another hug, a bigger one this time. "Don't worry about us. Really, we'll be fine."

She nods as she wipes her nose with a tissue. "Yes, I know you will."

"Take care, Mrs. Foster," says Leah cheerfully. "And thanks again for letting Emily come."

Mom nods again, then steps back, waving as we hand our boarding passes and IDs to the woman at the gate. "Have fun!" she calls out.

And it turns out that we do have fun. First of all, we put on our sunglasses as we wait at our gate for our flight, pretending that we're famous models—like we don't want anyone to recognize us. Of course, this is ruined when we don't get to sit in first class.

"Someday, I'll be sitting there," Leah whispers as we move through the section. I notice that she moves more quickly, more gracefully, while I sort of struggle not to bash people with my bulging carry-on bag, not to mention my hips.

We finally get our stuff stowed in the overheads and get settled into our seats. Of course, I can't help but notice how Leah must tighten her seatbelt to make it fit her narrow hips. I, on the other hand, have to loosen mine. I also notice that I completely fill the seat. I can't imagine how people who are heavier than me would manage to fit into these tiny seats.

That's when I see a very obese woman slowly moving our way. I notice how other people are watching her, looking at her with a variety of expressions, everything from disgust to fear (like they're worried she's going to sit next to them), and even pity. The woman eventually sits down across the aisle from us, but she has to push up the armrest and then fills up two seats. The flight attendant, who looks irritated, hands her a seatbelt extension. I glance away, embarrassed for this poor woman. But at the same time I'm thinking that could be me someday—if I don't watch out. Then, as I compare myself to her, I start thinking that I look pretty good. I lean back into my seat and smile to myself. Yeah, life could be worse. A whole lot worse.

And after we get to Chicago and check into the huge hotel where the two-week modeling school will take place, life does get worse. Infinitely worse.

It seems that all the girls signed up for AFI are (1) very pretty,

(2) very thin, and (3) very stuck up. And it's clear that I do not fit in.

"I shouldn't have come," I whisper to Leah as we wait in the registration area. "I don't belong here."

She shakes her head. "Don't worry about it, Emily. You'll be fine."

"Everyone is skinny," I tell her.

"Not everyone," Leah assures me as she discreetly nods toward an area where several more "average" type girls are hanging on the edges, as if they, like me, aren't comfortable with this crowd. The problem is that, unlike me, they're not overweight. Okay, they're not skinny either. But I would much rather be their size than mine. I feel like crying, or running, or maybe jumping out a window.

I'm not even sure how I make it through that first day. I can tell people are looking at me, just like that obese woman in the plane. Some are disgusted, some feel sorry for me, and others just can't figure out why I'm here. Neither can I. But, I tell myself, I'm doing it for Leah. I even convince myself that it's a spiritual sacrifice, like "laying down your life for a friend." Jesus said there was no greater gift to give. I just hope that Leah appreciates it. I also hope she knows that she owes me one now. Make that ten or twenty. She owes me big-time for this.

I try not to complain too much. I realize that I could totally ruin this time for Leah and, after all, it's her aunt who's paying for these two weeks of torture. So I pray a lot, at least to begin with. I continually ask God to strengthen me. And I believe that he does. I also pretend like this is just a big lesson in humility and that I will be a bigger person (hopefully not physically) afterward. I try to embrace a good sense of humor—mostly making fun of and laughing at myself, which I am getting rather good at. I don't hide the fact that the only reason I came was so Leah would get to come. And I think some people actually respect this and don't expect too much of me. Like I'm the homely chaperone and not really a student.

Ironically, some of the girls—the stunningly beautiful, sickeningly skinny girls—begin to accept me. In fact, I think they might even like me. Okay, maybe it's because they like how fantastic they look standing next to the fat chick. I don't know. Regardless, I do try to laugh and play along, and I never let on that I'm dying underneath. I feel like the modeling-class clown—the one with the sad face beneath the cheery makeup and big red nose. It's pathetic.

As the first week passes, I realize I am actually learning some things. I know how to use makeup to make my face appear thinner—how to highlight and shade areas to "sculpt" a more attractive look. I know about exfoliation, which is supposed to make your skin glow when you remove old, dead cells, but I'm hoping it will actually slim me down if I scrub hard enough. Who knows? I've also learned how to sit, stand, and walk more gracefully, and in a way that should make me appear thinner and taller, although I have my doubts.

But the biggest thing I've learned—the thing that could be the key to change—is how to *really* lose weight. There seem to be several foolproof methods, which these girls don't seem too concerned about revealing to me—probably because I am not the competition. And so I begin to experiment. Of course, I don't tell Leah about this, since she adamantly believes there's only one right way to do it. She continues to insist that a "healthy diet with lots of fruits and vegetables and whole grains, plus a moderate amount of daily exercise and lots of water" is the only way to safely lose weight. Well, hey, maybe it works for her, but I wasn't impressed with only losing three pounds.

I've come to accept that there is a secret formula to losing weight. Actually there are several ways, but I don't want to use drugs, so that leaves two that seem to really work: (1) You quit eating all foods except for green salads topped with lemon juice, and lots of diet sodas, or (2) you binge, eating everything in sight (when no one is looking), and then throw it up afterward (also when no one is looking).

Okay, this hasn't been exactly easy for me to accept these new eating habits. For one thing, food has been one of my best friends for quite some time now. How can I possibly give it up completely? Surviving on air (or salad greens and diet soda) like some of these stick girls do seems pretty unrealistic for me. Skipping a meal here and there, well, I'm finding that's doable. But then I'm so ravenous that I can't control myself at the next meal. So I binge. Really binge. I nearly emptied out one of the hotel's snack machines last night. Of course, I got rid of it shortly afterward. But then I felt guilty. I still feel a little bit guilty. Like what am I doing here? Didn't I use to think this was wrong? But I tell myself this is just an experiment—I want to see how my body reacts to a change like this. Who knows? Maybe it won't even work.

Another vital ingredient of this secret formula is that you must exercise fanatically, wherever and whenever possible. Even if it's just "fidgeting" as Leah calls it—because "as everyone knows, fidgeters burn calories." And burning calories is what it's all about. There are quite a few girls who religiously refuse to use elevators. Even though our rooms are all on the seventeenth floor, they will use only the stairs to get up or down. The first time I tried this, I had to quit after only five flights, and I thought I was going to die. I did a little better the second and third times. After almost a week, I can consistently get at least halfway up. My goal is to make it all the way up by the end of our two weeks. Some of the girls also rely on the fitness center and swimming pool during free times. I don't mind working out at the fitness center so much, but I refuse to get into a swimsuit in front of this crowd. Thankfully, I didn't even pack one, which provides a pretty good excuse.

So for the time being, I've designed my own weight-loss plan, which includes lots of exercise and alternating between starvation and B&B (binge and barf). Or, as a girl from Indianapolis puts it, I'm an "Ana Mia," which is a girl who uses both anorexia and bulimia, but I think she's overstating things.

I don't like to call these "diets" by their medical terms, because I don't honestly believe that's what I'm doing. Anorexics and bulimics choose a way of life. If anything, this is only a temporary situation for me—just a means to an end. After I lose my weight, which I'm now more determined than ever to do, I will follow Leah's example. I will eat and exercise sensibly. But until that time, I feel a need for drastic measures.

Some of the girls, the ones who seem to like me or like being seen with me, are even giving me helpful tips.

"Drink lots of coffee, it'll make you hyper and you'll burn more calories."

"Make sure you eat plenty of dairy products when you binge . . . it'll help to protect your esophagus when you throw up."

"Brush your teeth after barfing so the acid doesn't eat the enamel off."

"Use laxatives if you get tired of barfing. It's called purging and it cleans your body out."

"Take diuretics if you need to lose weight fast, like for photos."

Okay, some of this stuff was pretty overwhelming at first. But the more I hear, the more I get used to it.

After twelve days of alternately starving myself and binging/purging (since I still can't decide which method I prefer), I experience a little scare today. I am going up the stairs when I get so light-headed that I almost pass out. I actually see stars or fuzzy spots in front of my eyes, and I have to sit down right there on the stairs and put my head between my legs. I'm not sure how long I do this, but when I finally lift my head up, I do feel a little worried. I see that I'm on the fifteenth floor, and just to be safe, I decide to take the elevator up to my room.

Fortunately Leah and everyone else are still downstairs being fitted for the big fashion show tomorrow, the grand finale of modeling school (and I am playing hooky since I really don't want to participate, and because I have no plans to become a professional model, no one really cares whether I participate in everything anyway).

So, feeling a little worried about my health, in general, I go into our room to lie down for a few minutes. I immediately think I should pray, since that's what I usually do when I feel worried or scared or sick. But then I stop myself. It's like I can't pray about this, like I have this sense that if I pray, I will have to admit that what I'm doing is wrong. And, although I've felt sort of guilty about what I'm doing, I've been telling myself that it's not a sin.

I mean, aren't we supposed to take care of our bodies and treat them like temples? And having an overweight body doesn't exactly qualify, does it? Wouldn't God get more glory if I lost this flab and became fit? And so I go round and round until I finally come to the conclusion that this is probably just a lesson in self-discipline for me. For the past year or so, I've been careless about eating (or overeating), and I think that food has become far too important to me—like it is a god or something. And I know that God doesn't want that for me. So I decide that losing this weight really is the right thing to do. But I have to admit that it's still kind of hard to pray. Although I do manage to bumble along.

I start feeling better, and I think that God is answering my prayer. And suddenly I feel energized and I want to go down to the fitness center while most of the machines will be available, since the girls are probably still trying on clothes.

And here is the highlight of my day—perhaps of the whole time I've been here—since no one is around to see me, I get on the scales and weigh myself. And to my astonished delight, I have lost ten pounds! That's ten pounds plus the three I'd lost previously for a total of thirteen! I can hardly believe it and double-check to make sure I've got the weights in the right places. But it's true!

So now I know that these methods really do work. And while I'm sure that Leah meant well with her more careful weight-loss plan for me, I think she'd have to agree that this is better. Way better! Although I don't plan on telling her anytime soon.

But here's what totally rocks—I feel powerful. As I'm working out, and really going hard at it, I feel like I finally have some control over my life. Like I have the upper hand over my body now. Like I have really accomplished something—something big. And, I realize as I'm jogging on the treadmill, this is just the beginning.

I make sure to drink plenty of water during and after my workout. And then I even take the stairs again, without fainting this time. I shower and change (noticing my clothes are getting baggy!), and when I go back downstairs to join the other girls for dinner, which I've decided to actually eat and then dispense of, I am flying high.

"Why are you so happy?" Leah asks when I find her standing in line for the salad bar.

"I've lost more weight," I tell her.

"Cool!"

"Yeah," I say. "I guess you were right after all."

"See, I told you to just be patient. Project Swan is going to work."

I nod as I load up a plate with everything in front of me.

"But you're not really going to eat all that, are you?" she looks concerned.

"Well, I worked out for about an hour, and I never had any lunch," I say.

She considers this. "Well, I guess it's okay then."

"And I might work out again before bed," I add.

"Cool," she says. "Then I will too. I haven't even had a chance to exercise yet today."

There's supposed to be a speaker tonight—someone who Leah and everyone else are all gaga over—from some big New York modeling agency that I couldn't care less about. She steps up to the podium just as we're finishing dinner, and I use the opportunity to slip out to use the restroom. It takes less than a minute to rid myself of tonight's meal, but I wish I'd thought to bring a toothbrush. The idea of losing the enamel on my teeth is a concern. So I wet a paper towel and do my best to wash my mouth out. Then I go back out and pretend to be interested in what this elegant older woman has to say. But in reality, I'm just thinking about myself and how great I'm going to look in a swimsuit before long if I keep losing weight, which I will. And sure, maybe I won't look as hot as the girls here, although I personally think some of them are too skinny, but at least I won't be too embarrassed to go swimming this summer. Maybe I'll even look good in time for camp, although I can hardly believe that it will be starting next week. And I can hardly believe that I've lost thirteen pounds even before camp begins! Life is good.

And then, as I'm sitting there amid all these beautiful girls who are really hoping to make it as professional models, and I have abso-lutely no aspirations for anything like that at all, I am suddenly over-come with this huge sense of gratitude. So much so that I actually begin to pray silently in my heart, and I sincerely thank God for helping me to lose this weight. Seriously, it seems like nothing short of a miracle to me! What a high! And I think about how my parents will react to this new me—especially my dad. Maybe he'll start treating me the way he used to. Maybe this will fix things between us. I am full of hope!

seven

WHEN WE GET HOME FROM CHICAGO, LEAH AND I HAVE LESS THAN THREE days to regroup and get it together before it's time to head off to camp. But as soon as I get into my house, I am so exhausted that I end up pretty much vegging out for the remainder of the afternoon. Fortunately, Mom doesn't seem to mind. She's just glad to have me home. I'm still a couch potato with my bags piled in a heap in the family room when my dad gets home from work.

"Welcome back," he says in a slightly grumpy voice as he looks down to where I'm flopped on the couch. He stands there for a moment, carefully eyeing me.

"Thanks," I tell him, sitting up straighter.

"Have you lost weight, Emily?"

I smile. "Yeah, thirteen pounds last time I weighed."

Now he actually pats me on the head. "Hey, that's a good start."

Okay, I'm not quite sure how to respond to this "good start" business. I mean, I know he's trying to be encouraging, but couldn't he say something a little bit nicer? Does he have any idea how hard I've worked to lose this weight?

"Better get up and moving if you want to keep it off," he tosses over his shoulder as he heads to the kitchen in search of my mom.

I growl under my breath as I pry my tired body from the soft couch and gather up my bags, dragging them to the laundry room. I begin to toss dirty clothes into a hamper. Of course, I know Dad's right. I'm not stupid. If you want to lose weight, you gotta keep moving. It's what I've been beating into my head for the past few weeks.

So, despite the fact that I haven't had anything to eat since before our flight this morning, when I had one of those little boxes of Special K with skim milk, I force myself to keep going. Keep moving. Action equals burnt calories, burnt calories equal less fat. Keep moving, Emily. This will pay off. I take a walk around the neighborhood, planning to walk thirty minutes in one direction, which means it will take thirty minutes to get back. But I find it incredibly hard just to put one foot in front of the other, and it feels like miles and miles. When I finally get home, I just want to go to bed and sleep. Or eat maybe. But I'm trying not to think about food.

"Why don't we go for pizza?" Mom suggests just as Matt gets home from baseball practice. "In honor of Emily's homecoming."

"Works for me," says Matt.

"But pizza is fattening," my dad complains. "And remember Emily is trying to lose weight."

Matt rolls his eyes at me, like *welcome home, fatso.*

"But she's done such a great job already," Mom says, "maybe she needs to celebrate a little."

They go back and forth a bit, and finally I jump in, taking Mom's side—well, Matt's too, I guess. "Pizza would be great," I say. "Especially since I've been living on rabbit food lately. I think I deserve pizza for a change."

Dad's disapproval is written all over his face, but Matt and Mom both look pleased.

So pizza it is. Of course, I know exactly what I'll do after I finish consuming not only way too many pieces of pizza but a chocolate milkshake too.

"I don't know how you'll keep the weight off if you keep eating like that," Dad says with a creased brow.

"She took the last piece of pepperoni," Matt complains.

"Sorry, bro," I say lightly, then excuse myself to the bathroom. Thankfully, no one else is in there, and I quickly relieve myself of all that heavy food. And as Dad drives us home, I feel rather smug and even wonder why it took me so long to figure out how this weight-control thing really works.

Okay, by the time I go to bed, I have this pounding headache and a ringing in my ears that won't stop, and I do feel kind of sick to my stomach, which is odd since I know my stomach is empty. But after a shower, I get on the bathroom scales and discover that I've lost another pound, and I am so elated that I decide these uncomfortable side effects are a small price to pay for results.

The night before camp, Leah and I go to the meeting for camp counselors. Pastor Ray, the youth pastor, who already had us work through a short notebook, now gives us some camper materials and finishes off with an encouraging pep talk.

"The most important thing is to become a real friend to your campers," he says finally. "You want them to trust you and to believe you, so that when you share your faith, they will listen to you. But remember it's a balancing act, because you also need their respect. They need to understand that you are the authority in your cabin, and when you say no or give a warning, they need to know that you really mean it. Of course, if a serious problem arises, a senior counselor will step in. Most of all, we want you to all have a really cool time. And we want the name of the Lord to be lifted up and glorified." Then he closes with prayer.

"You up for this?" Leah asks me as she drives us home.

"I guess so. But I have to admit that it sounds a little intimidating."

"I think it's going to be fun. Did you see the guys from West Park there tonight? There was this one guy who looks like he could be Brad Pitt's younger brother."

I laugh. "Sorry, I missed that. But I did notice Brett McEwen was keeping an eye on you," I say. "Are you certain that he's really not that into you?"

She just shrugs. "I don't know. I mean, like I already told you, we didn't really seem to click on prom night. I mean, it was fun and everything, and we laughed a lot and stuff, but I don't think there's any real chemistry between us."

"Oh." I want to ask her if this means it's open season on Brett McEwen now, but I realize how ridiculous I would sound. I mean, yeah sure, someone like me would have a real chance with someone like him. You bet!

"Have you packed yet?" she asks as she stops in front of my house.

"No," I admit. "Did you plan on helping me again?"

She laughs. "Hardly. I haven't packed either. You're on your own this time, girlfriend."

"Thanks a lot."

But as I begin going through my stuff, I realize that quite a few of my clothes are getting pretty baggy, and I end up tossing a lot of them into a "fat" pile. Not that this is such a big loss, since I never had much success at finding cool clothes once I started piling the weight on anyway. I mean, it's hard to find cute things in fat-chick sizes. Not every store even carries them. Besides, I always wanted the kinds of clothes that would cover me up, kind of like fat camouflage, I guess.

I briefly considered begging my mom to take me shopping earlier today, but then I realized how I'd be dropping even more pounds before too long, so I might as well wait until I reach my goal before I invest too much money in clothes.

So tonight as I scramble to pack a few things, I have to dig a little deeper in my closet as I search for summer clothes. Buried beneath the clutter, I discover some items I'd previously "outgrown." And I begin to feel hopeful. I get really excited when I find this old pair of Gap shorts that I used to love. They're the kind of denim that's soft after lots of wearing and washing. I practically lived in these shorts about two summers ago, back before I packed on the pounds. I'm not even sure why I saved them really, but now I'm thinking it wasn't a mistake. Unfortunately, they're still pretty tight around the thighs, but at least I can get them on over my hips, and if I suck in my stomach, I can actually get them buttoned, even if the jelly roll hanging over my midsection does resemble a partially inflated inner tube — definitely not a good look. But in time . . .

I decide to pack the shorts anyway, as well as some other things that are on the small side. I guess I'm hoping that I'll lose another thirteen pounds during camp and that maybe they'll fit by the end of two weeks. Or maybe I'll lose even more than that. It's not like camp food is going to tempt me much. Besides, I've got the secret formula now. Why not go ahead and get as skinny as I can?

After I'm packed, and definitely traveling light as far as my duffel bag goes, I decide to check out some of the anorexia-bulimia websites that one of the model girls (a fellow Ana Mia) told me about in Chicago. She said these sites were full of great tips for taking off, and keeping off, weight.

But what I read tonight is both shocking and frightening. And I can tell that most, maybe all, of these Ana Mias are definitely not

Christians. They are taking this weight-loss thing to a much further extreme than I would ever want to go. Those girls seem really desperate, like being skinny as a stick is the most important thing on earth to them. I just want to lose a few pounds. In fact, once I can comfortably fit into my old Gap shorts again, I'll be perfectly happy. And I will quit doing this. I know I will.

My mom drops Leah and me at the church the next morning. Everyone is supposed to meet here at ten o'clock, and after a welcome speech by Pastor Ray, who's in charge of all six churches involved, we are immediately put into cabin groups. I have six girls (Penny, Chelsea, Hilary, Jenna, Kendra, and Faye) who will be in my cabin. Although only one of these girls (Jenna) is from my church and I barely know her, my first impression of the six is fairly positive. They seem pretty quiet and nice, and perhaps even a bit unsure of themselves. And I am pleased to see that they seem to like and respect me. I think it may help that I've taken off some weight and that my hair looks good. Plus I'm wearing the cool capri pants that Mom got me for the Chicago trip. This is going well.

We pile into the van. I take the front passenger seat, next to the driver, Mrs. Myers (she has a son in middle school), and I manage to wedge my guitar case in between us. And so far, I'm thinking this isn't too bad. I mean, how hard can it be anyway? For starters, I'm about five years older than these middle-school girls. I should know a thing or two about keeping things running smoothly. I should be able to hold this together. But we're barely out of the parking lot when I begin to suspect that there could be trouble.

"I don't want to sit back here," Kendra loudly complains when we're at our first stoplight. She's sitting between Penny, the overweight girl of the bunch, and Hilary, a Hispanic girl who has probably not spoken more than three words so far. Penny just looks out the side window as if she's ignoring Kendra, and Hilary has her nose in a paperback with a horse on the cover. "Come on," whines Kendra, "somebody better trade places with me or I'll get carsick and ralph all over you guys in front of me."

"I'll trade," offers Chelsea.

"Thank you," I tell Chelsea, and she grins at me, revealing bright silver braces across her teeth.

Kendra is barely in the middle seat before she makes some comment that's hard to decipher, but it doesn't sound very nice, and Faye starts to laugh loudly, glancing over her shoulder to the backseat, I'm sure to stare at poor Penny.

Jenna, a slim and pretty blonde, just rolls her eyes at me as if she knows what's up and questions my ability to handle it.

Then our driver asks if everyone is buckled up.

"We're good to go," I tell her, and she gives me a look that suggests maybe we're not.

"How about if we sing on the way to camp?" I suggest as I reach for my guitar case.

Kendra groans. "That's so juvenile."

"Yeah," agrees Faye, who I figure must be Kendra's cohort. "We did that back in kindergarten."

"I like to sing," says Chelsea brightly. And I'm thinking I *like* this girl.

"Me too," says Penny quietly.

"That works for me," I tell them as I take out my guitar and check to be sure that it's tuned. "I'm a little rusty because I just got back from Chicago," I tell them as I strum a few chords.

"What were you doing in Chicago?" asks Kendra.

Now I consider this. Do I dare tell these girls that I was at modeling school, of all places? I mean, it's obvious that I am *not* model material. Why set myself up for their scorn?

"Yeah," chimes in Faye. "What were you doing in Chicago, Emily?"

"I was there with a friend. She's a counselor too. Leah Clark."

"Oh, I know who that is," says Jenna. "She goes to our church and is really pretty."

"You mean that tall, thin girl with the long, dark hair?" asks Faye with interest.

"That sounds right," I say as I adjust a string.

"Yeah, I wanted *her* for my counselor," adds Kendra.

"Thanks a lot," I say as if I'm hurt, but then I laugh. "You're right, Leah is really pretty. She's also my best friend and we went to Chicago so she could take modeling classes."

"She's going to be a professional model?" asks Kendra with real awe in her voice.

"Maybe so," I say.

Then I start playing a goofy praise song from church, and after a few lines I think that most of the girls are actually singing along. Even Mrs. Myers joins in. Fortunately, the camp is only an hour away, and I really think that singing makes the trip go faster. But even as I'm leading them in songs, I feel a little worried. This could be a tough bunch. The way Kendra immediately set her sights on poor Penny—what if she keeps it up? How am I supposed to hold these girls together for two weeks, let alone be a "spiritual leader" like Pastor Ray expects us to be? *God help me*, I pray silently and sincerely, as I try to think of one more song to sing before we get there.

Finally we pull into the camp parking lot, and I am feeling pretty exhausted. I'm not sure if this is partially due to hunger or if it's the strain of being trapped in an automobile with six twelve-year-olds for more than an hour.

We unload our stuff and begin trudging up the small hill to our cabin, number 8 in the girls' section. Penny is lagging behind, and I want to go back and keep her company, but the truth is, I'm afraid that I might not make it myself. I don't know when I've felt so tired. I'm carrying my sleeping bag, my duffel bag, and my guitar, and I feel like every step is agony. But I call back to Penny, encouraging her to keep up and saying that it's not too far now. "We'll be there soon."

"She's too fat to keep up," I hear Kendra say from where she's walking with Faye up at the front.

If I had more energy, I'd run up ahead and give Miss Kendra a piece of my mind, but as it is, I am huffing and puffing myself.

Finally, we reach our little A-frame cabin. Naturally, Kendra and Faye are already inside, and they've picked out the best bunks—lower bunks against the back wall that are directly across from each other. They must've already heard that the bottom beds are much cooler on hot summer nights. Oh well, at least I get the counselor's bed, which is a single bed off by itself. Chelsea sets her things on the last remaining lower bunk, and when Hilary and Jenna arrive, they are forced to take upper bunks. But, thankfully, neither girl complains. Hilary goes for the bunk over Faye and Jenna takes the one over Chelsea.

When Penny arrives, I can tell that there is going to be trouble. She's staring up at the last available bunk, the one above big-mouthed Kendra, and Penny looks stressed.

"No way," says Kendra when she realizes what's going on. "She can't sleep over me!"

I give Kendra a warning look that doesn't even faze her.

"I mean it," says Kendra, holding her hands out for emphasis. "The whole bed could collapse and I would be killed. My parents would sue you."

Faye snickers.

"You can have my bed, Penny," offers Chelsea. I'm so thankful for this sweet girl that I could kiss her.

"Thanks," mutters Penny as she huffs over to the bed and dumps her stuff on the floor next to it.

"Whew," says Kendra. "That was close. I didn't want to wake up flatter than a pancake."

Once again, Faye laughs. These two are really pushing the limits. And, okay, I realize I'll need to do something about Kendra and her nasty attitude and mean mouth, but I'm so tired right now that all I want to do is just to lie down for a few minutes.

"You guys go ahead and unpack your stuff," I tell them as I sit on my bed and pull out the camp schedule. "It looks like there's nothing planned until lunchtime. And that's in about forty minutes. Five minutes beforehand, they'll blow an air horn to let us know to get down to the cafeteria." Then I flop onto my back and sigh loudly. I pray silently, desperately. *God, get me through these two weeks.*

eight

"HOW ARE YOUR GIRLS?" I QUIETLY ASK LEAH WHEN WE FINALLY RECONNECT at the end of the day. We're on our way to campfire and most of our girls are walking ahead of us. Except for Penny. As usual, she's lagging behind. I'm sure it's partially to keep a safe distance from Kendra and Faye. I've tried to drop hints to these two girls, as well as the whole group, but it's just not working, and I'm feeling like a complete failure.

"They're great," Leah says happily. "Real sweethearts."

"Oh."

"How about yours?" she asks.

"I don't know . . ."

But it's too late to continue our conversation. Two of her girls have come back to walk with her, one on each side, taking her hands as if she's their new best friend. It's hard not to feel jealous.

Counselors are supposed to sit with their campers at meals and at campfire, but already I have lost Kendra and Faye among all the middle-school kids. But at least my other four girls stick with me as we find an empty log bench and sit down. I search the crowd for my two runaways. Finally I see them with Leah and her girls. I try to catch Leah's eye, hoping that she'll send them back to me. But this isn't working, and finally I have to go over and get them myself.

"You guys are supposed to sit with your cabinmates," I tell them. They give me their best party-pooper looks as they reluctantly come back and sit with us.

The worship team, which includes Brett McEwen, does a great job with the songs, and then there is a little skit and some games, followed by one of the counselors giving his testimony. It occurs to me that this could be the one Leah's so into, the guy who looks a little like Brad Pitt. And when I glance over to where Leah is sitting and see the starry-eyed look on her face, I know I'm right: This must be the guy from West Park. I scan the crowd, trying to find where Brett McEwen went to sit after helping with worship. Finally I spot him, duh, sitting directly across from me. He seems to be looking my way, but since we're on opposite sides of the campfire, I realize he's probably just looking at the speaker. Anyway, "Brad Pitt" turns out to have a good testimony, and I figure this guy has more than just looks going for him.

Then it's time to return to our cabins for the night, and while I encourage my girls to stay together, I find that keeping Kendra and Faye with us is a little like herding cats. But eventually we are all safely back in our cabin, and I tell my girls to gather around for group time.

All the counselors have this workbook that we're supposed to stick to during our two weeks up here. It includes morning and evening devotionals that we're expected to do on a daily basis. I've already gone over mine and am ready to do it tonight, but I also feel the need to say something more first, something that might help my girls to be a little kinder to each other and maybe even bond. That's what I'm hoping for.

"You know, we're all coming from different places," I begin, thinking that I might actually have their attention, although it's hard to tell. "And we all have different problems and struggles. But I really hope that we can get close to each other during our time together at camp. And I think it would be cool if we could learn to understand and accept each other despite our differences. I hope by the end of this session, we'll really trust and respect each other for who we are." I look around the group and smile hopefully.

That's when Kendra suppresses a somewhat obnoxious giggle. Like she thinks I've just said something really funny. And of course Faye starts in too, and pretty soon both these girls are laughing so hard that you'd think I might have a future as a stand-up comic. And I am ready to knock their two silly heads together.

"Okay, do you want to let us in on the joke now?" I say, feeling very much like my third-grade teacher, old gray-haired Mrs. Snyder. That was one of her favorite lines.

Kendra simply shakes her head. And Faye, like monkey-see-monkey-do, follows suit. Penny, who's already sitting on the outskirts of this group, just looks away as if she suspects this has to do with her. Hilary pulls her knees up to her chin and looks at her feet, and Jenna looks exasperated and tired. Pretty much the way I feel right now. Why do they have to make everything so difficult?

I glance over to Chelsea, hoping that this sweet girl might be able to help me out of this mess, but even she looks to be at a loss right now.

"Is there any way we can switch cabins?" Kendra suddenly says in a snitty tone, interrupting the uncomfortable silence.

"Huh?" I look at her and try to figure out what she means by this. Then I glance around our cabin's interior to see if there's something second-rate about it, but everything seems to be in fairly good condition, for a cabin anyway.

"Can we?" she persists.

"Do you think there's something wrong with this cabin?" I ask. Of course, this just makes her start giggling again.

"Not the cabin," she says, using that snitty tone again. "Just the people in it."

Faye puts her hand over her mouth now, as if she's trying to suppress her own giggles, and the sound that erupts is like a snort, which makes Kendra laugh even harder.

"What do you mean by that?" I ask Kendra, knowing that I'm probably opening a great big ugly can of worms right now. But maybe it's better to just get this crud out in the open, deal with it, and get it over with.

She rolls her eyes as if it's obvious. "It's like you said, Emily, some of the people in this cabin are *different*." Then she glances at Faye, for support I'm sure. "And *some* of us don't really belong in this group. It makes us feel uncomfortable and we'd rather be some-place else where we fit in better. Isn't camp supposed to be fun? Anyway, can we switch?"

I take in a deep breath, feeling like I really don't need this right now. But here it is anyway. And my patience, unlike my waistline, has worn thin. "Kendra," I begin in a serious tone, and the cabin grows very quiet, "it's clear that you think you are better than the rest of us." I glance at her cohort. "And maybe you think that too, Faye. But I'd like to know just what is it that makes you two so much better. Why do you think you are superior to us?"

Kendra just shrugs, giving me a look that says, *Duh, isn't it obvious?*

But Faye glances away, like maybe she's a little embarrassed by my accusation. Good.

"Come on, Kendra," I urge. "Why do you think you're so special? What gives you the right to treat others like they're below you? Like you should be able to just walk on them? Can you tell the group, please? I'm sure we'd all like to know what makes you better." I glance around at the other girls and see a mixture of expressions, everything from extremely uncomfortable to very curious.

Kendra looks directly at Penny now. "Well, for one thing, *she* is fat." Then she looks at Chelsea, "and *she's* a geek," and then she looks at Hilary, "and *she* won't even talk to anyone," and then she looks at Jenna, and I can't imagine what she's going to say about the pretty girl, who hasn't rubbed anyone wrong as far as I can see. "And Jenna is anorexic."

Jenna stands up now, putting her hands on her slim hips and scowling at Kendra. "And you are just plain mean, Kendra. I hate you and Faye both! I hate all of you!" Then Jenna goes and climbs up onto her bunk, turning her back to us, and I think she's crying. This is going so well.

Hilary is hunched over with her head bent all the way down into her knees as if she's trying to turn into a ball, and Penny is starting to cry now, and I would like to strangle Kendra.

"Jenna is right," I tell Kendra. "You *are* mean. And you do think you're better than everyone else in this cabin, but you are so wrong. In fact, you couldn't be further from the truth. Did you know that Jesus said that people who want to be great should humble themselves? He said they should treat others better than themselves. And you're doing just the opposite, Kendra. Do you think Jesus would like how you're treating other people? Or maybe you're not really a Christian."

"I am too a Christian," she says in an angry voice.

"Then act like one," I tell her.

Now I look around the rest of the group. "Hey, I don't know you guys very well yet, but I'm really sorry that Kendra has gotten us off to such a crummy start."

No one says anything for several seconds. And I'm not sure what to do or say now. Can anything make this better? "Penny," I finally say, waiting for this poor girl to make eye contact with me, "I know how you feel. I really struggle with my weight too. I've felt like the fat girl lots of times. But I can tell that you're a really sweet person, and I can tell that you've got a sensitive spirit. And I'm really looking forward to getting to know you better." I smile, and to my relief, she smiles back, just slightly, but enough to give me hope.

"And Hilary," I say, waiting for her to pull her head out of her knees and look up, "I don't know you either. But I can see that you love to read, and I'm guessing you're smart too. And I just hope that you'll open up and let us get to know you better because I'm sure you're a really interesting girl. Can you do that?"

The corners of her mouth tilt up just slightly, then she says, "Okay."

"And Chelsea," I say with relief, "you have been my hero today. And I'm guessing that you take being a Christian seriously, because Jesus' love is so obvious in your life. And if I had to pick a second leader in this cabin, it would definitely be you. I hope all you girls will take the time to get to know Chelsea better, because I know this girl has something very special going on."

Chelsea looks slightly embarrassed, but then she gives us a big grin, and her silver braces just gleam.

Now I look at Jenna, or rather her back since she's still up in her bunk, still facing the wall. "And Jenna," I say loudly, hoping she'll turn around, "I know you a little from my church and I've always liked you, and I also happen to think you're a very pretty girl, but that's about all I know. And I'm sure there's a whole lot more, so I hope you'll let us get to know you better too."

She makes a little grunt so that at least I know she heard me. Then I turn my attention to Kendra's partner in crime. "Faye, I don't really know you, but you seem to be a follower, and it appears that you've fallen right into Kendra's control. But I think that underneath those giggles and smart remarks, you still feel a little bit guilty about being mean." I pause and give her a long, hard look. "Am I right?"

She kind of nods, keeping her eyes averted from Kendra's.

"Are you a Christian?" I ask her pointedly.

She nods again.

"Do you think Jesus would be pleased with the way you and Kendra have treated the girls in your cabin?"

She shakes her head and to my surprise, I see her chin quiver slightly and then a tear streaks down her cheek. "I'm sorry," she mutters.

Kendra makes a huffing sound, folding her arms across her chest in a very closed-off way. But I just ignore her as I lean over and put my hand on Faye's shoulder. "I'm sure that the girls you've offended will forgive you," I tell her, "if you're really sorry." She nods and wipes a tear. "Being a Christian is as much about forgiving others as it is about loving. And I have a feeling we'll get lots of opportunities to do both."

Then I take in a deep breath and look around the room, taking in each girl and her challenges. "So it looks like we all have some work to do during the next couple of weeks. None of us is perfect, and if anyone here thinks she is, she's sadly mistaken. Now, instead of doing devotionals tonight"—I reach for my guitar—"let's just sing a couple of songs and call it a night. I think we're all pretty worn out. Okay?"

They seem agreeable to this, so I lead a couple of songs about love and then recite John 3:16 to them, ending in a prayer for everyone in our cabin before I tell them good night.

I am totally exhausted when I fall into bed. And I feel like a failure. Not only did I fail to do devotions like we're supposed to, I know I have failed at getting through to Kendra. And the idea of spending two weeks with this girl is overwhelming. I feel like giving up right now.

Besides that, I feel hungry. Ravenous. I barely picked at my food during lunch and dinner today. For a short while, I considered binge-ing and purging, but then I realized that there's not a lot of privacy in these group bathrooms. And I didn't want to have to explain why I was "sick." But now it hits me that I probably won't be able to do a good job as a counselor and continue with my weight-loss regime. Besides that, I'm worried that Kendra will be onto me before long. And I wonder how she knew about Jenna. Or if she's even right. I pray once again before I go to sleep. I beg God to help me to deal with this stuff. The truth is, I really want to keep losing weight. And I certainly don't want to start putting the pounds back on. But at the same time I don't want to flake out on these girls either. I wonder how it's possible to have it both ways.

nine

I'D LIKE TO SAY THAT OUR LITTLE HEART-TO-HEART CHAT THAT FIRST NIGHT changed everyone and everything for our cabin and that life was beautiful after that, but unfortunately that is not the case. While things did go a bit better during the second day, we have some definite lines being drawn today.

Somehow Kendra has not only won Faye's loyalty back but she's managed to get Jenna to join the dark side as well. It makes me understand how leaders like Hitler won a following. Something about social cruelty and discrimination seems to be empowering. I'm a little surprised about Jenna, but I think her solidarity might have something to do with Kendra's anorexia accusation on the first night. Maybe Kendra's holding something she knows over Jenna to keep her under her thumb. But I can't be sure.

Mostly it's like having two cliques in the cabin. We have the "cool" girls, who are really the mean girls. Although in Faye's and Jenna's defense, it is Kendra who leads in the mean department. And we have the "geek" girls, who Kendra has assigned "secret" names. Penny is "Pig," Chelsea is "Brace Face," and Hilary is "Mouse."

"Pig always slows us down," Kendra complains to Faye and Jenna. Her tone is hushed and she thinks I can't hear since I'm a few steps behind, walking with Chelsea and Hilary. Penny trails behind like a caboose. I suppose what Kendra is saying is true. Penny does have a hard time keeping up and we're often late for things. But it still irks me to hear Kendra calling girls names behind their backs, and I'm worried she might do it to their faces when no counselors are around.

We get to the mess hall and, as usual, I am torn. I know that the food here is pretty high in carbs and fat, and yet I know I need to eat in order to maintain my stamina and keep up with these girls. I've been trying to do smaller portions, although it's still way more than I've been eating during the last few weeks. I've noticed how Jenna eats hardly anything, mostly just picks at her food, rearranging it on her plate, and despite Kendra's proclamation, Jenna seems to get away with not eating. No one has said anything more about her eating habits or her thinness. And I'm surprised at how desperately I want the freedom to do the same. I actually envy Jenna.

Meanwhile Penny goes for seconds and, if no one's looking, thirds. But the scary thing is how there's this part of me that wants to join her. I would love to just eat and eat—and then hit the bathroom and barf because I really don't want to look like Penny, and I know that I could. Mostly I just feel confused. Like when did eating and weight get to be such a life-consuming thing for me? And will it ever end? It's like this vicious cycle. Or maybe a trap. Whatever it is, I'm really starting to hate it. It's like I'm always off balance.

After lunch, just as we're exiting the mess hall, Penny starts screaming. "I've been stung!" she yells. "Help, I've been stung!"

I already know that she has a serious allergy to bees, so I tell the other girls to head down to the activity area while I rush Penny to the nurse's office, where her medication is kept in the fridge. I just hope that I won't have to give her the shot. I've been told how to do this, but I am definitely not good with needles. I'm afraid I'd pass out. Fortunately, the nurse is there, and within seconds, she administers the shot. I don't even watch.

"Penny will need to lie quietly for a while," the nurse informs me. "Can you wait here with her while I go check on the boy who sprained his ankle this morning?"

"No problem." She leaves, and I notice a scale behind her desk. I cannot suppress the urge to see how much I weigh. I feel like a thief as I tiptoe back there and get on it. Then, to my complete dismay, I discover that I've put on two pounds. Two whole pounds. I can't believe it. That's almost a pound per day. At this rate, I'll be right back where I started by the end of this camp! I have to do something!

And so I decide that even if it makes me tired, I will go back to not eating. It's the only way to keep this thing under control. Not only that, but since it's only been about fifteen minutes since I ate, I decide to go into the bathroom and get rid of it.

And here's the weird thing. After it's over, I feel empowered again. I feel like I have some control over my life and my weight again. And this somehow energizes me. I know it doesn't make sense, but it's the truth. I think, okay, I can handle this. I can handle these girls. I am going to come out on top.

I check on Penny now, wondering if she's ready to go yet. And I'm relieved to see that she's sitting up and seems fine.

"Feeling better?" I ask.

She nods then frowns. "How about you?"

"Huh?"

"It sounded like you got sick just now . . . in the bathroom."

"Oh." I had hoped she'd been sleeping. "Well, I'm kind of a wimp," I tell her. "Hypodermic needles and hospitals and all that medicine and stuff . . . it makes me sick to my stomach sometimes."

She nods as if she believes me. "Oh, yeah, that's just like my little sister. She just looks at a needle and practically passes out."

I laugh. "Well, I can relate."

Then we walk down slowly, at Penny's pace, to join the others.

"I wish I could walk faster," she says as she's huffing along.

"That's okay."

"I'm not used to walking so much."

"Yeah, we do walk a lot," I say. "But it is a good way to burn calories."

She nods. "Maybe I'll lose some weight."

We're about halfway down to the activity area when it seems Penny has slowed down even more. I turn and glance at her, concerned that she could be having another reaction, that maybe the shot didn't work. And I see that her face definitely doesn't look good. In fact, she seems to be in pain.

"Penny," I say suddenly, stopping in the path to really look at her. "Are you okay?"

She shrugs.

"Is it the bee sting?"

"No. That's not it."

Okay, she does seem to be breathing just fine. "What is it then? I can tell something is wrong."

She looks down at the ground, almost as if she's embarrassed. "It's my legs."

"What do you mean?"

"Where my thighs . . ." She stops.

"Huh?"

She looks around, as if to see whether anyone can see us, then pulls up her baggy shorts to reveal the inner section of her very large thighs.

"Oh my gosh!" I exclaim when I see how red and inflamed they are. It's as if someone has been beating her. "What happened?"

"They rub."

"Oh."

"That's why I have to walk so slow."

Now I put my arm around her shoulder. "Poor Penny," I say. "That looks like it really hurts."

"It does."

"I wonder if the nurse might have something."

"Do you think?"

"Wanna go back and see?"

She nods. And so we make our way, very slowly, back to the nurse's office, where she first cleanses then treats Penny's abrasions. She also gives Penny some antibiotic ointment to take with her. "And use ice packs," she advises as we're leaving.

"How can I do that?" Penny asks as we start trekking back down to the activity area again. "Kendra and the others would really make fun of me then."

I consider this and have an idea. "Maybe when we get sodas at the Snack Shack, you can ask for extra ice with yours, and when we sit down to drink them, you could set yours between your legs, to hold the cup, you know?"

She nods. "Yeah, that might work. Thanks."

By the time we get to the activity area, things are just winding down. It looks like they had relay races today. And I can tell that Penny is relieved. After this is free time, one of the few times during the day when campers are allowed to come and go as they please. Most of the kids, including the "cool" girls from our cabin, usually head for the pool to cool off. And although they never invite Chelsea, I've noticed that she has a good friend in another cabin (from her church), and these two athletic girls always seem to find something fun to do. Meanwhile Penny and Hilary head back to the cabin, where Hilary reads her books, and Penny takes a nap. I know this for a fact because I usually join them. It's my one break.

But today, I'm feeling energized. I'm thinking that my life is back on track and I'm going to keep losing weight. I want to get some exercise. And so I take myself on a little hike that I'm sure will burn off all the calories I consumed at breakfast. I tell myself that I'll take off those two extra pounds in no time because I'm back in control. I have the power to do this!

Okay, I do feel a little self-conscious at dinner, but I make sure to take small portions of everything except the green salad, which monopolizes my plate. And I even pretend to put dressing on. Then I take my time eating every bit of my salad, and I move the other pieces of food around until it really does seem like I've eaten, then I put my napkin over the uneaten food, and my plate looks pretty much like the others. I can do this!

I'll admit that I feel guilty. But I'm not quite sure why. I mean, it's not like God wants me to be fat. All I have to do is look at Penny to know that she's miserable. Is God pleased with that? I don't think so. But then I look at Jenna, and while she looks pretty and thin, she does not look happy either. And I guess this worries me.

As her counselor, I'm thinking maybe I should talk to her about her eating habits. I mean, it's one thing to eat like I am when you're overweight and trying to slim down. But Jenna is already thin. Maybe even too thin. She really should eat more. But how can I confront her without feeling slightly hypocritical? I ask God to guide me in this. I pray that he will use me with all these girls. Part of being a counselor is committing to pray for the kids in your cabin on a regular basis. And I am faithfully doing this. I even pray for Kendra. Okay, sometimes my prayers aren't so nice. But I think God understands.

On Friday, I sneak into the nurse's office under the guise of asking for some more ointment for Penny, which isn't completely false since she told me she's almost out. Fortunately, the nurse isn't even there, so I am able to get back onto the scale again and, to my relief, I have lost two pounds. I realize this is only breaking even, taking me back to where I was before I came to camp, but it's better than gaining.

I'm back to my old regime now, drinking lots of water, exercising every chance I get, and then pretty much not eating anything that has calories. I sort of miss the bingeing-and-barfing days, since there is something satisfying about actually putting food in your mouth and consuming it, even if only briefly. But I reassure myself that at least this will protect the enamel on my teeth. That's something. So, for the most part, I'm feeling pretty good, like I'm on top of things again.

Except for when it comes to the girls in my cabin. That's where I think I'm failing. I even brought it up with Pastor Ray. I told him about how divided my cabin was, how the "cool" girls were making everyone else miserable, and that I didn't know what to do.

He just smiled. "Don't be too hard on yourself, Emily. Unfortunately, this comes with the territory for most middle-school girls. There are always the ones who want to torture the others. But usually it's because they're feeling tortured themselves. If you can get the mean girls to open up, you might discover what's making them hurt."

"What if I can't?"

He just shrugged. "Then you can't. Just remember that God can. And he can use anything. Whether you can see it or not, there's probably something good that's going to come out of this."

"I hope so."

"And don't forget your best weapon."

"Weapon?"

"Prayer. When all else fails, or even succeeds, prayer can change things."

I thank him and tell him that I need to go get my girls from activity time. The theme for activities is "Survivor" (a spin-off from the reality show on TV). The tribes start out by cabin, then after each contest the director combines the tribes until eventually there are only two huge groups. We're still in the first stage, so the girls in my cabin are one tribe. Today is the water-challenge day, and I know that Penny is really worried about having to wear her swimsuit. She covered herself with a big T-shirt, but I know she's feeling very uncomfortable about actually getting wet. The funny thing is that Jenna, our skinny girl, also wore a T-shirt over her swimsuit. Unfortunately, I doubt that made Penny feel any better. I just hope that Kendra and Faye haven't been teasing her.

I consider what Pastor Ray said about prayer being my weapon. Maybe he's right. Maybe I haven't been praying hard enough. Or maybe my prayers aren't getting through. I vaguely wonder if this could have to do with the way I'm eating, or rather not eating. Because despite my justifications, I do feel guilty about it sometimes. Like, why do I have to be so sneaky if there's nothing wrong with what I'm doing? And why does it worry me when I notice Jenna glancing at me, as if she's suspicious?

But then I remind myself of how people fast and pray to get God's attention. Why can't that be what I'm doing? And so I decide that I will just look at it like this: I am simply fasting and praying for my girls. Shouldn't that make a difference? Shouldn't that change things?

ten

WHEN I FIND MY GIRLS, OR RATHER HALF OF THEM, I CAN TELL SOMETHING'S wrong. Penny is soaking wet and sobbing, and Hilary looks furious. Chelsea appears to be trying to comfort both of them.

"What's up?" I ask with some hesitation, unsure whether I really want to know.

"Kendra pushed Penny into the lake," says Hilary. "On purpose."

Chelsea just nods. "We had decided that Penny would be our dock person. We were doing a relay in the canoe and one person was supposed to stay on the dock and hand us the balloons."

I'm not entirely sure what they're talking about, but I just nod as if it all makes perfect sense. "And?"

"I already told them that I couldn't swim," says Penny. "And I can't. Well, not very well anyway."

"Yeah, and Kendra said that it wouldn't matter because she could probably just float," says Hilary, and I'm impressed with how involved she seems to be getting. I've never heard her talk this much.

"Yeah, Kendra just laughed and said, 'Blubber always floats,'" adds Penny as she pushes a limp strand of wet hair from her pudgy red face.

"She was being pretty mean," says Chelsea, the one girl who usually doesn't say a bad word about anyone.

"She was mad that our team wasn't winning," says Hilary. "I guess that was sort of my fault."

"You did your best." Chelsea pats Hilary on the back. "That's all anyone can do."

"So we were all done with the relay and Kendra walked by, real close to where Penny was standing, and then she pretended like she was falling and she slammed right into Penny and that's when Penny fell in the lake."

I sigh. "Too bad."

"Chelsea jumped in to save me." Penny turns and gives Chelsea a very appreciative smile. "She's the best swimmer in our cabin."

Chelsea kind of shrugs.

"Where are the other girls?" I ask. Not that I particularly care.

"The pool."

"Was it just Kendra then?" I ask, wanting clarification. "Is she the only one I need to talk to about this?"

"Yeah," says Penny.

"But Jenna and Faye were both laughing really hard," adds Hilary. "And they all made fun of Penny when Chelsea and I were trying to pull her out of the water."

I can just imagine this.

"They didn't even help," says Chelsea.

Well, this really makes me mad. I've had just about enough of Kendra and her meanness. And even though Pastor Ray told me how they hate to send kids home, he did admit that they occasionally had to. And as I storm over to the pool, I'm thinking maybe this will be an option. Maybe we can ship Kendra home. If nothing else, taking her up to the lodge to see Pastor Ray might get her attention.

"I don't want to go with you," says Kendra after I tell her what's up. The three girls have just emerged from the pool, and they are dripping.

"It's not your choice, Kendra," I say in a firm voice.

"But why?" she says in a whiny voice.

"Because you pushed Penny in the lake."

"That was an accident!" She glances over to Faye. "Wasn't it?"

Faye just nods without making eye contact with me.

"Not according to my witnesses," I say.

"I have my witnesses," Kendra tosses back. "Right, Jenna?"

I look over to where Jenna is standing, and that's when I notice that her wet T-shirt is clinging to her like plastic wrap, and beneath it I can actually see her ribs sticking out. And I feel shocked. As if she knows what I'm thinking, she immediately pulls her T-shirt away from her emaciated frame and she fluffs it out so that it's not so revealing.

"Right, Jenna?" Kendra asks again.

"Yeah," says Jenna, looking away. "It was an accident. Kendra lost her balance and Penny was in the way."

"And that's why you all laughed at her?" I continue. "And why none of you even helped her out?" Then I turn back to Kendra. "You can come with me now, or I can bring Pastor Ray back to make you come. Your choice."

So it is that Kendra comes. But you can tell by her posture and the way she stomps off that she is really ticked. But not as ticked as I am.

Neither of us says a word as we go up to the lodge. But I am trying to pray. Not that it's working too well. Instead of praying for Kendra, I find myself praying for Jenna. I am feeling extremely worried about this girl. Her anorexia looks serious. And I think I should say something to her. But what?

When I find Pastor Ray, I give him a quick explanation of the incident at the lake.

"It wouldn't be such a big deal," I say finally, "except that Penny, as you know, is extremely overweight. Everyone in our cabin knew she was freaked about wearing a swimsuit and terrified about getting wet. And besides that, she doesn't swim. What Kendra did was not only cruel but it could've been dangerous. If Chelsea hadn't jumped in—"

"Penny was floating," says Kendra impatiently. "It's not like she was going to drown."

"What if she was?" I look at her. "Would you have cared?"

"You're just making a big deal out of nothing." Kendra rolls her eyes. "It's probably because you relate to Penny more than to the rest of us."

I feel a rage bubbling in me, and I wonder how it is that I ever thought I was qualified to be a counselor to demonic girls like Kendra. "And why is that?" I ask in what I'm sure is a seething tone.

"Like you said the first night, you know how it feels to be the fat girl."

Now I turn from her and look at Pastor Ray in a way that I'm sure must be screaming, *Help me! Help me!*

"Emily, if you don't mind, I think I'll handle this with Kendra myself. I'm sure your other girls would like to have you back with them anyway."

"Thank you." I nod, then turn and walk away. I am still seething. And as I walk back to the cabin, I do pray. I pray that Pastor Ray is calling Kendra's parents right now and that she will be on her way home before dinner.

But when dinnertime comes and the girls and I head up to the mess hall, I am surprised and dismayed to see that Kendra is already there. It seems that she was assigned to KP during free time this afternoon.

"Thanks for getting me into trouble," she says as she joins us.

"It was your choice to push Penny into the lake," I remind her.

Then she gathers Jenna and Faye and starts telling them how unfair everything is and how she hates camp and hates me and how she wishes they *would* send her home. This makes me think that perhaps Pastor Ray brought up this possibility. Maybe it's not too late. I find myself hoping that she does something really bad—and soon—and that she will even wear out Pastor Ray's patience and be sent home. I even consider praying for this.

After the blessing is said, I begin my familiar routine of putting lots of green salad on my plate and very little of everything else. I'm thankful that the camp cook is so fond of green salad. But as I'm pretending to add dressing, I sense that I'm being watched, and when I set the dressing aside and look up, I see Kendra's narrowed eyes on me. And I can tell she knows.

What's the big deal? I ask myself as I pick up my fork. There's no law against dieting. And that's what I'm doing. Then I look across the table to where Jenna is sitting and I remember how awful her ribs looked beneath that wet T-shirt. And I know that I have some responsibility to say something. I'm just not sure what, or even how to. And, again, there's this feeling of hypocrisy. Like, who am I to confront Jenna?

As we're leaving the mess hall, Leah catches me and invites me to sit down and chat for a few minutes as our girls head over to the Snack Shack, where kids not only get their hits of junk food but actually do a little preadolescent flirting as well. I'm sure they won't miss us a bit.

"How's it going?" she asks. "I saw what happened with Penny at the lake. That was too bad."

I nod. "Yeah. Can you believe how mean some of these girls can be?"

"Yeah, I can, actually. Don't forget that I used to be the fat girl too."

I shake my head. "Yeah, that's right. It seems totally unfair that the way we look matters so much. I mean, why can't we just get over this gotta-be-thin-and-beautiful thing? Why can't we just accept ourselves and others for what we are?" I turn and look at my beautiful, thin friend—the same girl who has made me green with envy at times—and I have to laugh at myself. "Like I should talk, huh?"

"But I do know what you mean."

"I'll be so glad when camp is over," I confess. "I'm an abysmal failure at this counselor business. Can you believe that I actually thought this would be a good place to connect with cool Christian guys?"

She laughs. "Actually, it hasn't been too bad . . ."

"You mean Brad Pitt?"

"His name is Tanner. Tanner Olson."

"And?"

"And I think he's kinda into me."

"No way."

"Yeah. We've talked a few times, and he's even written me a couple of notes."

"Notes?"

"Yeah. He's kind of a poet."

"Seriously?"

"Shhh. It's not like everyone needs to know about this."

"Tanner the poet is into you." I just shake my head in wonder.

It figures. I mean, here I am working my tail off, trying to help the misfit girls to feel better about themselves, and trying to keep the "cool" girls from making us all totally miserable, and my best friend has not only got a bunch of really sweet girls in her cabin but she's also got this very cute and seemingly nice guy interested in her. Life is so unfair.

"He asked for my phone number," she's saying now. "He wants to get together when we get home. Can you believe it?"

I just shake my head again.

"Don't be down," she tells me. "I know that your girls are a challenge. But I'll bet things are going to change. I have a feeling God is really using you with them. And it makes sense that you'd get the tough cabin, Emily."

I frown at her. "And why exactly is that? Was I born under an unlucky star or cursed as a child?"

She laughs. "No. God probably knew that you had the maturity and strength to deal with something like this."

I sigh. "I don't think so, Leah."

"You're going to be fine, Emily," she says lightly, but I see her eyes looking over toward the Snack Shack, and when I turn to see what she's looking at, I realize it's Brad—make that Tanner. And he is waving at her.

"Love calling?"

She grins. "I just want to go say hi. Do you mind?"

"Not at all."

"Hang in there, Em." She pats me on the back. "And, hey, I almost forgot to tell you—you're looking great. Looks like you're still losing weight. Way to go!"

Before I have a chance to thank her, she takes off and I'm left sitting by myself on the bench. I take in a deep breath and tell myself to just enjoy this quiet moment of solitude. Who knows what our cabin time will be like tonight? I'm pretty sure that Kendra has her sights set on me now. I better watch out.

"Hey, Emily," says a male voice from behind me.

Surprised that any guy here besides Pastor Ray would actually know my name, I turn around in time to see Brett McEwen walking toward me.

"What's up?" I ask, as if it's no big deal that this guy is talking to me.

"This seat free?" he asks as he flops down beside me.

"Actually, I was thinking about charging for it. Twenty-five cents."

He laughs, then digs in his shorts pocket until he finds a quarter, which he hands to me. "There you go."

"Thank you." I pocket the quarter.

"I hear your girls are trouble," he says.

"Man, word gets around, huh?"

"Well, I was talking to Pastor Ray . . . I've got a couple of guys that make me wanna punch something. He mentioned that you've been having some challenges too."

So we sit there and swap war stories for about twenty minutes, and I can't believe how much better I feel when we're done.

"I think I should give you back the quarter," I say.

"Why?"

"In payment for that little therapy session."

He laughs.

"Seriously, it's comforting to know that I'm not the only one going through the wringer. That little bit of information might actually help me get through cabin time tonight instead of jumping in the lake."

"I know what you mean."

"Of course, even if I survive cabin time, they might find me dead in my bed by morning. Kendra gave me the evil eye during dinner, and I keep having these visions of her suffocating me with a pillow while I'm asleep."

He laughs even louder now. "Yeah, they should take out special life insurance policies on counselors with problem kids."

"I'm sure my parents would appreciate that."

"Well, keep the quarter," he says. "I had a good therapy session too."

Then the horn goes off, which makes me jump. That means there are thirty minutes until campfire. Just enough time to herd the girls to the cabin for sweatshirts and remind them to use the restrooms and brush their teeth. (For those who believe in this practice—I've heard some of the middle-school boys don't brush their teeth for two whole weeks—*eeuw!*)

"Hey, Emily," Brett says before we part ways. "Why don't we make a pact to pray for each other? Like when things get tough with your girls, you pray for me, and I'll do the same for you when my guys start making me crazy."

"Awesome idea!"

Now he sticks out his hand as if he wants to shake on it. "Deal?"

I take his hand and we shake. "Deal." Okay, I know it's just a handshake between friends, but I actually get goose bumps.

"Cool. See ya, Emily."

And so, as I gather up my girls and we head back to the cabin, I am feeling way better than before. It's like I'm totally high. Even when Kendra takes a jab at me for taking too long to brush my teeth, I barely even react. I actually smile at her, revealing those pearly whites, and say, "Hey, isn't it worth it?"

Okay, Em, I tell myself as we all parade down to campfire in our usual formation (Kendra, Faye, and Jenna bobbing around like fireflies up ahead of us, pausing now and then to complain about the slowpokes, Chelsea walking with me, and Hilary and Penny trailing along just a little behind us), *don't get all carried away by this little development. Brett is just being nice to you. Maybe he feels sorry for you. If anything, he just wants to be friends and prayer partners. No big deal. Just chill.* Even so, I am walking on air. And I am keeping that quarter as a keepsake!

eleven

I WISH I COULD SAY THAT THE SECOND WEEK OF CAMP GOES BETTER THAN THE first, that the girls all mellow out and begin to open up and share, and when it's all said and done, we go our separate ways feeling even closer than sisters. Unfortunately that's not the case. And now I know that it's totally my fault. I am a failure as a counselor.

All week long, Kendra continues to pick on the "geek" girls (as she calls Penny, Hilary, and Chelsea). Of course, she mostly does this behind my back, although I do catch her occasionally. And Faye begins imitating Kendra until she's as big a headache as her evil leader by the last day of camp. Jenna never says much one way or the other, but her allegiance is definitely with Faye and Kendra.

As a result, our cabin times are the absolute worst. I try to take the girls through the devotions, but other than Chelsea (my hero) no one really speaks much or opens up. If I hadn't brought my guitar with me, I'm not sure what we'd do to pass the time. But I tell myself as we sing worship songs together that maybe God can reach these girls through music. I know I can't seem to reach them through anything else.

But the day before camp ends, things get really ugly, and all I want to do is go home or just crawl under a rock somewhere. I guess I could blame it on the heat (it's in the high nineties) or on the fact that we're all a little tired, but that's probably a cop-out.

It starts during lunch. I can tell that Jenna isn't feeling too well. It's like she's been slogging along all morning. Then, after picking at her food and not eating, she leaves lunch early and goes outside to lie down on a bench. Feeling worried, I follow her and ask if she's okay.

"Yeah," she says, slowly sitting up. "Just tired I guess."

Okay, I know this might be my best chance to talk to her, since I am totally convinced that she's not only anorexic but also in danger. I caught her partially dressed once, and she was nothing but skin and bones. Really scary. Especially when you consider she is only twelve and not even fully grown yet. I can't understand why a girl her age would fall into this stuff.

"Jenna," I say quietly, thankful that no one else has left the mess hall yet. "I know that you're anorexic."

She doesn't say anything, just looks down at her thin little legs poking out of a pair of shorts that look too big. Jenna wears T-shirts layered over tank tops, so you don't always notice how skinny she really is.

"And I'm worried about you. Do you have any idea how this can destroy your health?"

Now she turns and looks at me, but instead of looking ashamed or contrite, she has an accusatory expression. "You should talk."

I shake my head. "Yeah, it's true that I'm dieting, trying to take off a few pounds, but you and I are different, Jenna. What you're doing is—"

"Different?" she shoots back at me. "You mean because you're fat?"

Okay, this hurts. But it's not like I'm not used to it. "Yeah," I tell her. "Because I'm fat, therefore I can afford to eat less. But you're—"

"I'm fat too," she says quickly, folding her arms across her chest.

And I have to laugh. "Yeah, right."

"I am. And I used to be way fatter." She turns and looks at me now, as if she's trying to guess how much I weigh. "I used to be kind of like you."

"But can't you see that you're way too thin now?"

She just shakes her head.

"Jenna," I say in what I hope is a sympathetic tone. "This is really unhealthy. Can't you see that? Can't you see that you're hurting yourself by not eating?" I hear voices and footsteps behind us now and I know that lunch is over, but I don't want to let this go. "Maybe you and I could go talk to the camp nurse," I urge her. "I'm sure she could tell you about anorexia and how it's not—"

"Why don't you go talk to the nurse?" she tosses back at me, standing up defiantly. "You're the one who's anorexic, Emily! I've seen what you do with your food. You're the one who needs help!"

Now Kendra and Faye are by Jenna's side, like reinforcements.

"How can she be anorexic?" asks Faye in disbelief. "She's fat."

"A fat anorexic," says Kendra like it's a big joke. "Is that what you call an oxymoron?"

"Oxymoron?" shrieks Faye. "That sounds nasty. What is that?"

"A fat anorexic," says Kendra in explanation.

Now it seems like all the campers are standing around listening, and some of them are laughing. Even Brett is there with his boys. I feel so humiliated that I just want to die.

But I just shake my head and stand up. Without saying anything, I walk off. And even though it's not time yet, I head down to the activity area. Sure, I would like to just go hide somewhere or simply pack my bags and leave this place. But I know I have a job to finish, and I am determined to do it. I may be a lot of things, but I'm not usually a quitter. And even though there are tears of embarrassment streaming down my cheeks when I reach the deserted activity area, I tell myself that I can survive this. And I remember my prayer pact with Brett. Okay, I'm still feeling totally bummed that he just witnessed that humiliating scene between Jenna and me. But it's not like I can change that. It's not like I can change much of anything.

So I sit down on a rock and tell myself to pray for Brett, and yet when I try to pray, it's really hard. It's like I've forgotten how, or maybe it's more like a part of me is shutting down or fading away—a deep spiritual part. Now more than ever I feel like a total hypocrite, a loser, and a fat, pathetic geek. Really, who do I think I am to confront Jenna about her eating disorder when I'm dealing with the exact same thing myself? And even though I've rationalized my behavior, excusing myself because I really am overweight, deep down I know that what I'm doing to my body is wrong. But I also know that *I don't want to stop.* More than anything, I still want to lose this weight. That's the only thing that's driving me right now. It's like I've left God completely out of the equation. And I have a feeling that God isn't too pleased with that. And that makes me feel even more guilty. Yet there's nothing I can do about it. I feel stuck.

So what do I do? I get up and start exercising. Like a fanatic, I put myself through the obstacle course several times, until I am hot and sweaty and panting like a dog. Then I go and refill my water bottle, still my constant companion, and I drink it down like it's food. Do I feel good? Not really. But I do feel empowered. And maybe that's enough. I tell myself that I'll get through this. Life won't always be this way for me.

By the time the kids start trickling down for activity time, I feel like I'm in control again. And I almost don't care what anyone thinks about me. If anyone confronts me, I'll just deny what Jenna said about me, and I'll point out that she's obviously in serious denial about her own problems and that she was simply trying to switch the focus from her to me—like a big smoke screen. I think that's pretty believable.

But things only get worse during activity time. Because it's the last whole day at camp, the activities director has a pretty full program planned—still based on the Survivor theme. The two tribes will face their biggest challenges today. It's funny, but as I stand watching on the sidelines, I feel like I'm playing a Survivor game of my own, just hoping that I can survive twenty-four more hours with these girls and this torture without totally losing it.

Anyway, for some reason, Kendra, Faye, and Jenna are really stoked about this (I'm pretty sure it's a boy thing), and they are determined to clean up in today's challenges. Not that the other three girls in my cabin don't care about it. In fact, Chelsea (the most athletic of the whole group) probably has the best chance of anyone to actually win.

But I can still tell that Jenna isn't feeling well. She looks paler than usual and isn't moving very fast. A part of me says that I should intervene, make her sit down and rest and drink some juice or maybe even take her to the nurse, but another part of me is still burning from her embarrassing accusations, and for that reason I just ignore her.

Suddenly, I hear someone yelling my name. Faye. She and Kendra are standing over someone. I run over and see that Jenna is lying on the ground. Her eyes are closed and she's not moving.

"She just fainted," says Kendra.

"Yeah," says Faye. "She finished the obstacle course and then she fell down. We thought she was faking it."

I'm kneeling beside her now, putting my face close to hers, and it doesn't seem like she's breathing. "Help!" I scream loudly. "Someone call 9-1-1!" Before I can do a thing, the lifeguard steps in and immediately assesses the situation and begins CPR.

"Move away," someone is saying. "Give them room!"

And then a small group of campers and counselors gather together, and they begin praying out loud for Jenna.

I feel like I'm watching everything from a distance and in slow motion, although I know that I'm standing only a few feet from Jenna. But it's like I can't move, like one of those dreams where your feet are stuck in cement. Without praying or barely even thinking, I just stand there like a statue, watching as the nurse steps in to assist the lifeguard in CPR, and before long there are paramedics and all the bystanders are cleared away as Jenna is transported to the emergency vehicle.

"Is she going to be okay?" Faye is asking me as the sirens fade in the distance.

I blink and look to see that all the girls in my cabin are standing around me now, waiting, I suspect, for me to say something reassuring, something to make them feel better.

"I don't know," I say.

Then they all begin talking, speculating over why this happened until finally Kendra, the consummate leader, proclaims, "It's all because of the anorexia."

The group gets quiet, waiting for her to go on, tell them more.

"I told you guys on the first day that Jenna was anorexic," she says in that know-it-all voice.

"How did you know?" asks Faye.

Kendra rolls her eyes. "Well, you saw how skinny she was. And she never ate anything. Like duh."

"Yeah, but some people are just skinny," says Faye.

"Not like that," says Kendra. "Jenna *is* anorexic. And she probably had a heart attack or something."

"I think we should pray for her," says Chelsea. And to my surprise, no one disagrees. And we actually gather in a circle and Chelsea leads the prayer. Okay, not everyone prays out loud, including me, but Chelsea does an amazing job, and I'm pretty surprised when Penny prays, but I am shocked when Kendra actually prays—and sounds sincere.

Things seem to settle down, and the activities director decides that it's time to end Survivor, proclaiming a tie between both teams, and no one argues. Then it's free time, and I am so exhausted that I head back to the cabin and sleep until it's almost time for dinner. What a great counselor!

At dinnertime, we learn that Jenna is okay. She experienced heatstroke and is being treated for extreme dehydration.

"Jenna won't be back at camp, since they plan to keep her in the hospital for a few days," says Pastor Ray. "But her family appreciates your continued prayers."

I sense that my girls are watching me at the table tonight, as if they're trying to figure out whether I, like Jenna, am also anorexic—the fat anorexic, or oxymoron as Kendra puts it. So to convince them otherwise, I eat more than I've eaten all week. And then I excuse myself, telling my girls that I have to go talk to one of the counselors about campfire tonight, and I go to the restroom and make myself throw up. In light of all that's happened today, I feel totally pathetic as I rinse out my mouth and splash cool water on my face and even apply some lip gloss. But I couldn't help it.

On my way back to the mess hall, I am stopped by Brett. And for some reason I feel certain that he knows what's up, that he knows what I've been doing. I'm also sure that my face looks totally guilty.

"Hey, Em," he says in a friendly tone. "Man, you've had a hard day today."

I nod. "Yeah. Kinda epic."

"I think you were right on about Jenna," he says. "Everyone's been saying that she really is anorexic."

I feel a small wave of relief. "I was trying to get her to go see the nurse," I tell him. "I was worried about her." I feel close to tears now but take in a deep breath instead.

He puts his arm around my shoulder. "You did what you could, sis. It's not your fault."

"Thanks," I tell him. "But I still feel totally bummed."

"I know. That's why I was a little worried about what I'm going to ask you. Feel free to say no."

Now I'm really curious. Maybe he's realized that he's actually as much in love with me as I think I am with him. Maybe he wants to ask me to marry him, to run away from here and live on a tropical island together. "What is it?" I ask, hoping that I don't look overly dreamy or spaced.

"Well, you know how Ed Simmons has been playing guitar with me at worship? Well, he had to leave a day early for his sister's wedding, so we're short a guitar tonight. I heard that you brought yours . . . would you be willing to help out?"

"Seriously?"

"Are you up for it?"

I consider this as I look into those deep-blue eyes. "Sure," I say. "Why not? I may totally blow it and end up looking like a complete freak. But, hey, it's not like that's anything new. And I seriously doubt that my life can get much worse after today."

He laughs. "That's one way to look at it." Then he pulls out a piece of paper. "Here's a list of the songs. Thanks, Em."

"Don't thank me yet," I warn him. "It could be a total disaster."

He just shrugs. "Whatever."

I like that he's been calling me Em. And as I head back to where my girls are just leaving the table, it occurs to me that what I said as a lie ended up being true. I was going to talk to one of the counselors about campfire, I just didn't know it.

I suppose the only thing that really goes right during this last week of camp is worship time at campfire. Fortunately, I know all the songs on the list, and I manage to play without embarrassing myself. Even Pastor Ray is impressed when he thanks me afterward.

"I didn't know you were that good," he says.

I kind of shrug. "Well, I mostly play for myself. Although I've been playing for my cabin a lot. Kind of helps us to get through cabin time."

He nods and pats me on the back. "You've had a hard time of it, Emily. But if it's any consolation, we think you've been doing great."

I want to contradict him on this but decide to just let it go. "Thanks," I tell him. "But I'm still glad that it's over tomorrow."

He laughs. "Hey, you're not the only one."

Everything after that is pretty anticlimactic. I think everyone in my cabin is relieved to say good-bye the next day. Other than Kendra and Faye, I don't see anyone exchanging phone numbers. Whatever.

"How you doing?" asks Leah when we meet up in the church parking lot.

"I've been better," I tell her.

"Poor Em." She pats me on the back.

"But at least it's over." I see Mom's car coming down the street in front of the church, and it takes all my self-control not to just jump for joy. I so want out of here.

"Hey, Leah," yells Tanner as he comes running toward us. "I almost didn't get to say good-bye to you." Then he grabs her into a big hug, actually swooping her around in a circle. Very romantic.

Feeling awkward, I look away, and I suppose I'm wishing that Brett would come up and tell me good-bye like that. But then I get real. I'm not stupid. I realize that it's not like that between us. Oh, in my dreams maybe, but I have no delusions. I know I'm not really the kind of girl that someone like Brett would get seriously interested in or want to date. He goes for pretty girls, skinny girls, cool girls. I know that I don't fall into that category.

Well, not yet, anyway.

twelve

"CAN'T YOU SEE YOU'RE TOTALLY NUTS?" I STARE AT MY BEST FRIEND AND wonder when she first started to lose her mind. Nearly a month has passed since we got home from camp, and admittedly we haven't been spending much time together. But that's only because I've been working full-time at a bookstore that's owned by one of Mom's friends, and of course, Leah has a boyfriend. Or maybe I just haven't been keeping up. But she's just informed me that she has a breast-reduction procedure scheduled for *the day after tomorrow*. Apparently it's been scheduled since May. Talk about honest communication between friends.

"That's exactly why I didn't tell you sooner." She just shakes her head. "I knew you'd act like this. I knew you wouldn't support me."

"But it's outrageous. Your boobs are perfectly fine, Leah. You do *not* need breast-reduction surgery. And I cannot believe your dad is really letting you do this." Okay, that's not totally true. I can sort of believe it. I just don't get it. Why would he allow this?

"Well, if it makes you feel better, Dad's not real thrilled. But Aunt Cassie understands. And she helped get him on board. She's so great."

"And then what's next?" I say, feeling sarcastic. "Maybe get a nose job, get your cheekbones—"

"What's wrong with my nose and cheekbones?" Leah rushes over to my mirror to peer at her reflection.

"Nothing." I roll my eyes. "That's just the point. Like how far do you plan on taking this stuff? I mean, I saw this woman on a TV show. She was in her thirties and she'd had about fifty different kinds of plastic surgery. And do you know what she looked like?"

Leah, still studying her face from various angles, shakes her head.

"She looked like a Barbie doll!"

"Yeah, right."

"She did, Leah. Even her daughter thought she did. And that was her goal. She *wanted* to look like Barbie."

Leah laughs and turns around. "So was she pretty?"

"No. She was freaky. Seriously, if I saw her on the street, I'd be scared. She looked like an alien. And her face looked like it was made of plastic. Really weird." I use my fingers to hold up the corners of my eyes then pooch my lips out to look puffy. "Kind of like this."

"Hey, maybe you should get your lips injected with collagen, Emily. You might look good in bigger lips."

"*Puh-leez.*" I flop back down onto my bed and pick up the July issue of *In Style* magazine that Leah brought, along with several other fashion rags that she's addicted to. Her goal, of course, was to show me photos of thin models with tiny boobs in order to convince me that she really needs the reduction surgery. However, I'm not convinced. Because for every flat-chested model she's shown me, I found one who was stacked. "Probably implants," she noted. "It's really unusual for skinny girls to have big boobs."

"Then you're just really unusual," I told her. But to no avail.

"This surgery is important to me," she says as she studies a glossy ad in *Vogue*. "I really hoped that you'd be supportive, Emily. Recovery is going to take some time, and it'd be nice to have a good friend to hang with, you know, to come over and comfort me." She holds up the magazine. "Isn't she beautiful?"

I shrug. "You know that model probably doesn't even look like that in person. You know how they touch up the photos and airbrush everything. She's probably dog ugly in real life."

"She is not," insists Leah. "I read an article in *People* about this girl, and she even let them use an untouched photo just to show what she actually looks like. And she was still really pretty."

"No zits or bags under her eyes or anything?"

"Not that I saw."

Now I go over to the mirror to study my own face. I even pooch my lips out again, still thinking about Leah's suggestion that I get my lips injected. And to my surprise, I think she might be right. I might look good in bigger lips.

"Do you think it hurts very much to get your lips done?"

"I don't think so. Becca had it done. You could ask her."

"No, I'm not really serious."

"Why not?" She looks closely at me now. "I actually think it would look great on you."

"Well, for one thing, it's probably really expensive."

"I thought you were getting rich working at the bookstore."

"Yeah, right. Like I want to blow my hard-earned summer money on lip injections. How stupid would that be?"

"You might be able to work out payments. That's what I'm doing for my procedure. Of course, I had to put half of it down. But Aunt Cassie covered it for me. She said it's an investment in my future. But lips would be cheaper. You could maybe work something out to like fifty bucks a month."

"Thanks but no thanks. Buying big lips on the installment plan . . . can you imagine how my parents would react if I did something like that? They would totally freak. And they'd never agree to sign for me in the first place."

"Well, you can do it when you're eighteen if you want."

"I think I'll pass. Besides, the injections would involve needles, right?"

"Yeah, but they probably use anesthesia so it doesn't hurt."

"Just the same, I still think I'll pass. The freaked-out-parent factor is enough to make me want to just say no to plastic surgery. Seriously, they'd probably refuse to pay for my college or something. They're just not into stuff like that. In fact, I'm sure they're going to think you're crazy for having your—"

"Please, don't tell them, Emily." She tosses the magazine aside and gives me this pleading look. "I really do want to keep this *top secret*. I'm telling everyone that I'm getting my tonsils out next week."

"Seriously?"

"Yeah. I don't want people to make fun of me."

"Don't you think people will notice the, uh, difference?"

"Not really. I mean, I wear a bra that pretty much holds them in anyway. I swear if my bra strap ever broke it could probably put an eye out."

"What about Tanner? You don't think he'll notice?"

"No, I don't." Leah glares at me. "And it's not like I've let him touch them, Emily. For your information, he's not even like that. And neither am I. Thanks for asking though."

"I wasn't saying that." I get defensive now. "I just meant he might've noticed how they look. I mean, even nice guys have eyes in their head. And you wore a swimsuit at camp. And it didn't exactly hold you in, if you know what I mean." I don't remind her that lots of the guys, including the middle-school boys, were ogling her figure.

"Well, I'll just deal with that later," she says. "My plan is to pretend that my tonsillectomy has some complications, like maybe I have an infection or something, and consequently my recovery takes longer."

"And it doesn't bother you to lie about this?" Now I'm surprised that I'm saying this, considering that I've been a little dishonest about some things myself, including my less-than-traditional weight-loss technique. I even lied to Leah when she started questioning me about it. I don't know why she was getting suspicious. But I know she'd be upset if she knew the truth.

"Yeah, it does bother me a little. But I think God will forgive me."

I don't respond to that, but I'm thinking, *Okay, so we go ahead and intentionally sin, knowing that God is loving and kind and that he'll forgive us anyway. What's wrong with this picture?*

"Okay, enough about me, Em. One of the reasons I brought these magazines over is so we can continue working on our swan project."

"But I haven't reached my weight goal yet," I remind her. "I thought we were waiting for that."

"You're so close, Em." She studies me now. "It's amazing really. I can't believe how well you've done, and how quickly. But are you really doing it the way I told you to? Are you eating lots of fruits and vegetables and whole grains? Because, I don't want to offend you, but your skin tone isn't exactly glowing, you know?"

"Huh?" I go back to the mirror and examine my face again. "What's wrong with my skin tone?"

"You seem kind of pale to me. Maybe you just need a really good facial," she suggests. "That'd be a fun thing for us to do while I'm recovering from surgery. That is, if I can talk you into coming to visit me. Will you still be my friend after I get my breast reduction?"

I laugh. "Yeah, Leah. It's not like I love you for your boobs. Sheesh."

"Okay, back to you now. We need to work on your image. And you've been so busy with work that the swan project got pushed aside. So far, all you've done is change your hair and lose weight—and believe me that's fantastic—but we need to work on the whole picture." She gives a tug to the baggy T-shirt I'm wearing. "Starting with your clothes."

"I thought I wasn't going to get any new clothes until I reached my goal."

"But you look awful going around in stuff that's either too big or out of style. You've dropped, like what, about three sizes?"

"I don't really know for sure." I get up and go stand in front of my full-length mirror. "But at least I can wear my Gap shorts now."

"Yeah, and they look pretty good. The thing is, you wear them all the time. Honestly, the last few times I've seen you, you have them on. I'll bet they'll be falling apart before long."

I check out the rear to make sure they're not too threadbare. "So what's the plan?"

"We need to go shopping—soon."

"When?" I look at the alarm clock by my bed. "You've got a date with Tanner in a couple hours. And I work all day tomorrow. And then your surgery is on Monday."

"I guess we'll have to wait until I recover. But that's something to look forward to. In the meantime, we can figure out what kind of stuff we should look for. Because we have to get clothes that look really great on you. You have to look totally hot by the time school starts."

I check out my thighs and frown. Sure, they've slimmed down some, but they're nowhere near as slender as Leah's. "How many pounds do you think I have to lose to get rid of these thunder thighs?"

She laughs. "Those aren't thunder thighs, Em. You just have a different shape, that's all. And different people carry weight differently. Really, I think you're looking great. Are you still exercising daily?"

"Of course." I don't admit that I exercise more than once daily, or that I walk to work or during my lunch break (instead of eating). In fact, I've come up with a new rule: Whenever I'm hungry, it's time to exercise and drink water. Oh, I do eat a few things now and then, but only things with very few calories. And I never binge and purge anymore. I decided that's too messy and too risky. And going more than two weeks without it convinced me I just didn't need the hassle.

"Then there might be some things about your body that you'll just have to accept, Em."

I turn and look at Miss Perfect. "You mean like the way you're accepting your bra size right now?"

"Hey, that's different. I want to be a professional model. This is career related. It could be the difference between really making it or not having a chance. Even Aunt Cassie agrees."

I wonder what Aunt Cassie would recommend for me. But I don't think I'll ever ask. It would probably involve about a million dollars' worth of surgery. And I'd probably end up looking like that Barbie-doll woman on TV. *Eeeuw.* Still, I wouldn't mind getting my lips done—if it wasn't so expensive and if my parents didn't know and if it didn't involve needles.

"Is there any other way to make my lips look bigger?" I ask.

"Like something I could do with makeup?"

"Of course, there are lots of tricks. And that's the other thing I wanted to talk to you about. We seriously need to work on your makeup. This, uh, natural look you got going isn't really working for you, Em."

"Well, I don't want to look all made-up either."

She stands next to me in front of the mirror. "Okay, look at me, Em. Do I look all made-up to you?"

"No, you look good—and natural."

"Well, we can make you look good and natural too. You just have to be willing to learn the tricks, and then you have to take a little time to do them. We need to get you into some routine beyond just lip gloss, mascara, and blush. I mean, don't get me wrong, that was a great start and a big improvement for you. But there's a whole world of cosmetics out there."

"Hey, I thought I was doing pretty good just to get that down."

"Yes. But you can do better."

I think about Brett now, and I think about my plan to totally wow him when school starts in September, which is barely more than a month away now. "Yeah, "I tell her." You're right. Maybe we can work on that during your recovery too."

"This is going to be fun, Em. And it'll help me to pass the time."

"How long does it take to recover anyway?"

"The doctor said to expect a week of downtime, and then the stitches come out."

"Stitches?" I make a face.

"Duh. They have to make incisions if they're going to remove—"

"Stop, stop!" I hold up my hands. "Too much information."

"Yeah, yeah. I almost forget what a wimp you are when it comes to medical stuff. Really, it's no big deal. I plan to be back to normal by the second week."

"Good." I want to ask her if there's any danger, any side effects. But the whole idea of someone slicing into your breasts makes me feel kind of sick right now, and I'm thinking maybe I don't really want all the gory details. I just hope that I can keep it together enough to visit her during her recovery time.

thirteen

On Monday, I stop by Leah's house on my way home from work. It takes about an hour to walk there, but I figure that'll help work off the whole milk that Frieda "accidentally" put in my sugar-free iced mocha during my afternoon break today. I usually have skim, which she is well aware of.

"Uh-oh," she told me after I'd already consumed most of my drink. "Looks like I blew it on your mocha, Emily." Frieda works at the coffee bar that's in the back of the bookstore. And sometimes I think she has it out for me.

"Blew it?" I closed the magazine I'd been perusing and looked up from where I was sitting at the counter minding my own business.

"I used whole milk." Then she gave me this cheesy smirk.

I frowned at her, wondering if this was really an accident or just plain sabotage.

"Hey, it's not like it's going to hurt you, little Miss Skinny Mini."

Okay, this made me laugh. But I know the only reason Frieda called me by that ridiculous name is simply because she is very obese herself. I'm guessing she weighs like 250 pounds, maybe even more.

"I don't know why you're always getting sugar-free mocha

anyway. You don't need to lose weight, Emily."

"So does that give you the right to sneak extra fat into my mocha? And for all I know, you haven't been using the sugar-free syrup either."

"It was just the milk. And, really, it was an accident. I'm sorry."

I could tell by her expression that she really did feel bad. "It's okay," I told her. "No big deal."

"But, really, Emily. I don't think you should worry about your weight so much. It's not healthy."

"I don't *worry* about my weight," I lied. "I'm just on a diet. I've lost almost forty pounds already. And I only started in May."

"What diet are you on?" She leaned forward, studying me with real interest. "South Beach, Atkins, low-carb, low-fat, what? I mean, I've tried most of them. And, well, you can see they didn't exactly work."

"It's not any of those." I stall, trying to think of an answer.

"What is it then? What's it called? Do we carry the book for it?"

"No, it's not that kind of diet. There isn't a book. I just try to eat less and exercise more, you know. And I try to avoid things that have fat or sugar."

"Doesn't that include just about everything edible? Like what do you live on anyway? Lettuce and broccoli and diet pop?"

I didn't admit that she was just about right. Instead, I lied again. "No, you can eat lots of things on this diet. Things like fresh fruits and vegetables and whole grains. And fish and chicken are okay and stuff like skim milk and low-fat cheese and yogurt. It's not really that complicated." As I said this, I told myself that I would start eating just like that — as soon as I reached my goal.

She nodded. "That sounds doable."

"Yeah," I told her. "You really should try it."

"Maybe I will. Especially since it's obviously working for you.

I'd give anything to look as good as you do."

It was kind of shocking to hear someone say that about me. I mean, I am usually the one who wants to look like someone else—like Leah or Becca or Lindsay Lohan (even before she lost the weight). Like the tabloids, I used to wonder if Lindsay was anorexic, but I've heard that she claims it was a big fat lie. And who am I to not believe her? Anyway, I thanked Frieda and wished her good luck with dieting.

"Maybe we can do it together," she said suddenly. "I mean, like eat lunch together and encourage each other."

"Oh, I don't know . . ."

"I noticed how you always leave for lunch. Is there a place you go to eat that serves the kinds of foods you're talking about?"

"Actually, I just grab a quick bite that I eat on the run, then spend the rest of my lunch hour walking."

"You walk for an hour?"

"Yeah. It's great exercise."

"But it's been so hot out. I think it's supposed to be in the nineties today. Did you walk during lunch today?"

"Yeah."

"And you didn't get baked?"

"Maybe a little. But I make sure to drink lots of water. That's really important to losing weight too."

"I hate drinking water."

"Oh."

"Maybe your diet won't work for me."

"Well, maybe there's one that will, Frieda. Everyone is different, you know."

A customer was waiting now. "Yeah," she said in a discouraged-sounding voice as she went to take his order. "You got that right."

As it turns out, Frieda got the temperature right too. I think it really is in the nineties as I walk over to Leah's house. The pavement is so hot that I can feel it through the soles of my shoes.

"You look hot," Leah tells me when I join her in their family room. It looks like she's been camping in here, lots of pillows and magazines and rice cakes and remotes and stuff.

"You mean like hot *good*? Or hot like I'm sweating like a pig?"

"I mean like hot *fried*. Your face is all red like you've been running or working out or something. Are you okay?"

"Yeah. I just decided to walk over here from work. And it's pretty warm outside."

"You walked all the way? Isn't it like five miles to town?"

"Probably not." I glance at my watch. "It took me about an hour."

"Well, go get yourself something to drink. Kellie made some iced green tea that's pretty good. Why don't you bring me some too?"

"Sounds good."

I pour us both tall glasses of iced tea then hurry back to join Leah. "How are you feeling?" I ask as I hand her a glass.

She takes a slow swig then lets out a little groan. "Awful."

I frown. "Really?"

"Yeah." She looks at the clock on the mantel. "It's probably about time for another pain pill."

"Want me to get it for you?"

"Sure. I think Kellie put them in the kitchen. She's been playing nursemaid all day since my dad can barely stand to look at me right now. And even though I appreciate her help, I was so glad when she finally decided to go home. I assured her you'd be here soon and that I'd be fine."

I set my tea on the coffee table. "I think I saw a prescription bottle by the sink. I'll go see if that's it."

I return with Leah's pills and wait as she takes one. I don't really want to look at her chest area, but I guess I'm a little curious. She has on a striped blouse, but it's not buttoned and beneath it I can see that she's wrapped in some kind of white gauze bandage that's got some yellow stain on it. She's also using an ice pack. But my general impression of her is *eeuw*. Of course, I don't let on.

"Did everything go okay?" I ask as I sit back down and pick up my tea and try to focus on her face instead of her bandages.

"I guess."

I take a sip of tea and then nearly spit it out. I didn't think that it would be sweetened, since Leah usually just makes it straight. But this is really sweet and it tastes like *real* sugar, not the fake no-cal stuff that I'm used to using.

"Something wrong with your tea?"

"It's sweetened with sugar."

"Yeah." She rolls her eyes. "Kellie always makes it like that. But after my surgery and not eating much, I figure a little sugar won't kill me. And the way I feel right now, maybe I wouldn't care if it did anyway."

I set my barely touched tea back on the table in front of me. "Are you still glad you did it?"

"I don't think that's a fair question right now. Ask me in a week or so."

"Okay."

So we talk awhile about other things. I tell her how Frieda called me Miss Skinny Mini at work. This makes Leah smile. "Well, you have lost a lot of weight, Em."

"I told her about your dieting tips, and she's going to try it too."

"Good for you."

After a while, Leah notices that I still haven't touched my tea. "I thought you were thirsty, Em. You should drink that."

"Well . . . the sugar, you know."

Her brows lift. "It's not going to hurt you. I mean, you just walked for an hour in the hot sun. Go ahead and drink it."

"I don't want it."

"Fine. Go get some water then. Just don't sit there looking like you're going to melt on me or even faint from heat exhaustion. Remember what happened to Jenna at camp?"

"Yeah." So I go exchange the tea for water and come back for the third time.

"Emily?" she says as I polish off the water in practically one long gulp.

"Huh?"

"What's up?"

"What do you mean?"

"I mean with you."

"Huh?"

"Well, I was just sitting here thinking about how little Jenna got heatstroke that day. And I also remembered how she accused you of being anorexic. I mean, I kind of forgot about it when the poor girl almost bought the farm. Talk about freaky. Anyway, I'm curious. I want to know why Jenna accused you of being anorexic. What was up with that anyway?"

I just shrug. "I think I'll get some more water."

But when I come back, Leah is still stuck on this. It's like she won't let me off the hook until I confess to her. "Come on, Em, we've always been honest with each other. I can tell something's up. Don't hold out on me. If you can't tell your best friend, who can you tell?"

"Like the way you didn't tell me about your surgery?" I try.

"I did tell you. I told you last May. But you were so totally against it that I really didn't want to go there for a while. I decided to wait until it was almost time. And then I told you, didn't I?"

"Yeah, I guess."

"So, come on, Em, time to come clean. Is it anorexia or bulimia or both?"

Maybe it's the heat, or maybe I'm just tired of hiding, or maybe I feel sorry for Leah all bandaged up like that, but I spill the beans. And to my surprise it feels kind of good to admit what's going on with me. And I remember how I've heard that admitting you have a problem is the first step in changing. Maybe that's what's happening with me. Although I'm not entirely sure that I want to change—not yet anyway.

"Well, I can't say I'm too surprised," she says, closing her eyes as if she's still in pain.

"Are you okay?"

"That pill will probably start working in a few minutes."

"Maybe we shouldn't talk so much," I suggest. "Maybe you should—"

"No." She opens her eyes. "I want you to listen to me, Emily. You're my best friend and I want you to stop the anorexic thing, okay?"

I consider this. Stop it? Just like that? Like I walk out of here and start eating like a normal person again? Even if I wanted to, I'm not sure that it's actually possible.

"I'm serious, Em. You know better than this. You're playing with fire."

"I plan on stopping it—"

"When?"

"When I reach my goal."

"No." She shakes her head. "You need to stop it now. It's dangerous. And so is the overexercising. You're stressing your body. And you could actually have a heart attack."

"Oh, I doubt it."

She sighs, then closes her eyes again.

"I shouldn't have told you all this," I say quickly. "It's just making you feel worse. I'm sorry."

"The only thing you should be sorry about is for what you're doing to your body, Em. It's all wrong. Please, stop doing it."

"I told you, I will. But I just need to lose about ten more pounds first. And I know this is the only way I can do it. You told me yourself how bodies are different, Leah. And I just wasn't losing weight when I did it your way. And we were doing the swan project and I wanted to be in shape in time for our senior year. Remember, we were both going to look hot for our last year. And I'm doing it, Leah. You should be happy for me." I ramble on a little more and her eyes remain closed. And finally I stop talking, and it gets very quiet in the room.

"Leah?" I say softly. But she doesn't answer and I realize that she's fallen asleep. Probably from the pain pill. And maybe it's for the best. Maybe the pain pill will help her to forget what I just said to her. Maybe my confession will be wiped away, and by tomorrow, everything will be the same as before. I can only hope.

I tiptoe from the family room in search of her dad, finally finding him in the laundry room.

"Sorry to bug you," I say, "but Leah's asleep now and I'm going home. Just in case you need to check on her or anything."

"Thanks," he says as he arranges a shirt on a hanger. I have to smile because I still think it's funny seeing a dad doing laundry, but then I know he's been doing stuff like this for years. Mister Mom. "And thanks for coming over to see her. I know Leah appreciates your support."

"Well, I wasn't in favor of the surgery, but I do love her."

He nods as he picks up another shirt. "Leah said that you and I were in agreement on that."

"I just hope she feels better tomorrow."

"I do too." He shakes his head as he shakes out one of Leah's little T-shirts. "I just don't understand why you girls think you have to look like the cover of a fashion magazine. It's not healthy, you know. And Leah's already beautiful enough. And you are too, Emily."

"Thanks."

He frowns now. "It sure looks like you've lost a lot of weight. I hope you're doing it carefully. Not taking any of those diet pills, are you?"

"No way. I've heard they're dangerous. This is just from dieting and exercise."

"Well, don't overdo it. You girls need to ease up on yourselves. Just enjoy life for what it is and be thankful that God gave you all that he did. Things could be worse." His eyes look sad, and I remember how his wife died of cancer.

"Yeah, you're right, Mr. Clark. I'll try to remember that."

"Good." He shakes out a towel. "Now, I didn't see your car out there, Emily. You need a lift home?"

"No thanks. I don't mind walking. It's probably cooler out by now anyway."

He frowns again. "Well, just remember what I said. Don't overdo it."

I smile brightly at him. "Don't worry, I won't. I just want to be healthy is all."

"Well, healthy is good."

And as I walk home, I try to make myself believe that what I'm doing is healthy. And that it's good.

fourteen

I visit Leah after work for the next couple of evenings, but she doesn't seem to get any better. And by Thursday morning, I find out that she has an infection and has been admitted into the hospital.

"I'm just so worried about her," Mr. Clark tells me. "I was hoping you might come by and cheer her up, Emily."

"Sure," I promise. "I'll come by on my lunch break."

But when I see Leah, I can tell she's in pain. Not only that but she's really discouraged.

"I never should've done this," she tells me with tears in her eyes.

"It's going to get better," I assure her.

"No. It was a mistake. I should've been happy with what I had. My breasts might've been a little bigger than I wanted, but at least they didn't hurt like this." Tears are streaming down her cheeks now. "Why was I so stupid?"

"You thought it would help your career," I say weakly, not even convincing myself.

"Yeah, right. Now I may end up with big ugly scars."

"Scars?" I try not to make a face.

"Yeah. When you get an infection it complicates the healing and you can scar."

"Oh." I hand her a tissue.

"The only way to get rid of the scars is more surgery."

"Oh."

"I am so stupid." She loudly blows her nose.

"No, you're not, Leah. And this is probably just the worst of it. I'll bet that you'll be feeling better by the end of the week. Your dad said they're giving you some pretty strong antibiotics that will whip this in no time."

"I just feel like such a fool."

"It's going to get better," I say as I hand her another tissue. Then I try to change the subject. I start talking about the shopping we're going to do once she's out of the hospital. And then I hold up my bag and pull out the new September magazines that just showed up in the bookstore. "Hot off the press," I tell her.

Her eyes brighten as I hand her the heavy edition of *In Style*. "Don't hurt yourself lifting it."

"Thanks, Em. You really are a lifesaver."

We try not to talk about her "ruined" breasts as we look at pictures and Leah points out what she thinks is cool or not and what might look good on me or her. And before I know it, it's time for me to go back to work.

"I'll come back after work," I promise. Fortunately, the hospital is only a few blocks from the bookstore. "Want me to bring you an iced mocha?"

"That'd be great, Emily. Thanks so much!"

And when I come back after work, she seems in better spirits, and we don't talk about her botched breast job or what the outcome may be. And, to my relief, she doesn't mention my "eating disorder" as she called it the other day before she went into the hospital. It's as if we've made some sort of silent pact not to mention these things.

Like it's just the price we must pay for beauty, and perhaps by not talking about these things, somehow that will make them okay.

Leah is released from the hospital on Sunday morning. And I go to visit her at home later that afternoon.

"Did you go to church today?" she asks.

I make a kind of guilty face. "I slept in."

"Oh."

"It's just that I've been getting up early all week, for work, you know. And I thought I was going to get up and go to church . . . but I just didn't wake up on time."

"I was wishing I could've gone to church today," she says in a kind of wistful tone. "I wanted to ask God to forgive me and to thank him for helping me to get better."

"But you don't need to go to church to do that."

"I know. But it just would've felt good. Because I really feel like God is teaching me something, Em, and it's almost like I want to let other people know."

"What do you mean?"

"I mean all this focus on how we look on the outside. It's just all wrong."

I nod without speaking, but I guess I'm feeling kind of surprised.

"When I was alone in the hospital, feeling totally rotten, and even wondering if I could die from the infection—which is actually possible—I asked myself how I'd feel if I was standing before God, you know, like waiting to be let into heaven. And I imagined him saying, 'Okay, Leah, what brings you here today?' And that I had to tell him that I had a boob job that went bad. And how embarrassing would that be? I mean, it's like I wanted to keep this whole thing top secret, and the next thing I know I'm standing in front of God and the whole world. And I just felt so incredibly stupid. Like how could I have been so shallow and vain?" Then she just looks at me, like somehow I should have the answer.

"I don't know."

"Well, I've decided that I'm going to change some things, Emily."

"Like what?"

"I'm not sure. But for one thing, I am going to quit focusing on the outside Leah and start working on the inside."

I nod. "That sounds good."

"And I'm going to spend less time reading stupid fashion rags and more time reading the Bible."

I nod again. But even as I nod, I feel this wave of frustration washing over me. Like I'm not quite ready to lose my fashion-minded friend yet. I mean, she hasn't even finished the swan project with me. How can she suddenly turn into this totally spiritually minded person when I still need her to help me look better? Of course, I can't say this to her. Like how shallow and selfish is that? Especially when she's having her own epiphany.

"I know it probably sounds silly . . . I mean after I've been so consumed by all this stuff. Talk about your one-eighties."

"What about your plans to become a professional model?" I ask meekly.

She just shrugs. "I don't really know. And I'm not sure that I really care."

"So, do you think that fashion and beauty are sinful?"

She seems to consider this. "I'm not really sure, Emily. I just think that getting obsessed with it is wrong. I can feel that inside of me. And trying to make myself look like something I'm not . . . well, that was wrong too."

I swallow hard and look away.

"But I can't judge you, Emily. I mean at one point, I was all ready to give you a big old sermon about not eating. And then I realized that would be wrong. Even though I'm seriously worried about your health, and I even feel partly to blame, you've got to come to God about this on your own. You've got to ask him to help you through this stuff, Emily. That's what I'm praying for you."

"Thanks," I mutter. But a part of me is saying, "but no thanks."

During the next week, I visit Leah a couple of times. And she still seems like a changed person. And for some reason it really irritates me. Like how can she do this to me? Finally, on Friday, and after she's had her bandages removed and is starting to do a few things, I decide it's time to say something.

"So my swan project is over then?" I'm trying to sound like it's no big deal, but I think she can see through me. "I work hard to lose all this weight with this big expectation that you're going to make me look really hot for our senior year, and then you just check out on me by exiting the fashion world completely?"

She frowns. "I don't plan to exit it completely, Emily. I just don't want to be obsessed with it." Now she looks at me and actually starts to giggle. "Not that you have that exact problem." She grabs the loose waistband of my khaki pants and gives it a pull, which causes the safety pin holding them up to pop open. "These are like two sizes too big for you, Em."

I nod. "That's my point. I am seriously fashion challenged, and you promised to help me out. Am I supposed to go it alone now? Just figure it out for myself?"

"No," she says, laughing. "That would be all wrong. Just because I need to tone it down in that area doesn't mean that you have to go around looking like a bag lady."

"Thanks a lot."

"Let's hit the mall tomorrow," she says.

"You sure you're ready?" Now I feel guilty. I mean, here she is just barely recovered from her surgery and infection.

"Yeah. Of course. And this will be a good test for me."

"Why?"

"Because I'm not going to let myself buy anything for me. I'm not even going to look. We're just going to focus on you."

"Yeah, I guess that will be quite a change."

She laughs. "Was I really that bad?"

"No . . . but I can just remember a lot of times when I trailed you around the mall, watching you trying on the coolest stuff and looking totally hot. This will be different."

"Guess it's about time."

"Are you going to see Tanner tonight?"

She nods with a grim expression.

"Are you still going to tell him the truth?" She told me that she's going to confess everything to him, including how she lied to him about the tonsillectomy and how her reduction surgery got botched, and how God's gotten her attention through all this.

She nods again. "I have to."

"Well, don't worry, Leah. I'm sure that he won't care. He should just be glad that you're okay. Right?"

"I hope so."

But the following morning when I pick up Leah to go shopping, she looks so bummed that I immediately suspect something is wrong.

"How'd it go with Tanner?" I ask as she gets in the car.

"Not good."

"Oh."

"I mean, he was understanding and everything. And he thought it was really sweet that I confessed the whole thing to him. And I know he felt bad for me."

"Well, what then?"

"He just has a problem with the whole surgery thing."

"Huh?"

"It kind of weirded him out."

"Oh."

"He thought maybe we should take a break, from dating, you know."

I don't totally get this line of reasoning, but instead I say, "Maybe that's good."

She sighs. "Maybe . . . but it feels like it's going to be more than a break, like it's really a breakup. I could see it in his eyes, Emily, it's like I repulsed him."

"Oh."

Now she starts to cry. Not the big huge blubbering kind of crying like she did that day in the hospital. But even so, it breaks my heart. Poor Leah.

"It's going to get better, Leah," I say.

She doesn't say anything.

"Just remember to breathe," I tell her, for lack of anything better.

Naturally, this overshadows our shopping trip. But somehow, Leah manages to help me find just the right things, and despite her pain, I am feeling pretty good by the time we stop for lunch.

"I'm buying you lunch," says Leah as we head for the food court. "And you're going to eat."

I'm not ready to argue with her. Especially since I know this girl has already been through a lot. "I'll try," I say as she leads us to the Chinese-food counter.

Leah orders a stir-fried combination with pork and fried rice, and I'm about to order the stir-fried veggies with no rice when Leah interrupts. "She'll have what I'm having," she tells the girl behind the counter, giving me a look that says, "Don't mess with me."

They quickly fill our orders and we go sit down, and to my surprise, Leah actually bows her head. "Dear God," she says, "thank you for this good food. We ask you to bless it and to make our bodies healthy as we eat it. Amen!" Then she looks at me with a challenging expression as she holds up her chopsticks. "Let's eat."

I slowly break apart my chopsticks and begin picking around for pieces of broccoli and celery and peapods. Anything green.

"Come on, Emily," she says in a less-than-patient tone. "You can do better than that. Try a piece of meat."

I swallow hard and tell myself that I can do this as I pick up a piece of pork. I even put it in my mouth before the gag reflex kicks in and I have to spit it out in the napkin.

Leah is frowning now.

"I'm sorry," I tell her, "but honestly, I haven't eaten meat in months. And it just felt so yucky."

She nods. "Okay, then just eat the veggies, including the carrots and onions—and, yes, I know they have carbs. Tough. And then you can work on the rice."

For whatever reason (maybe it's her breakup with Tanner or her rough week after the surgery or even the good help with clothes shopping), I really do want to please her today. And by the time I'm finished, I have eaten all of my veggies and about half of my rice. "Okay, that might not look like much," I tell her, "but it's the most I've eaten in months."

She nods with a sad expression. "I believe you."

"And now my stomach hurts."

"I'm sorry. But it's probably just stretching a little."

"Oh, great." I imagine it stretching out to the size of a watermelon.

"All you had were vegetables and rice, Emily. That's not going to make you fat."

I act like I believe her, but all I want to do is rush to the bathroom and make myself hurl. Unfortunately, I know that she would follow me in there, and then I'd never hear the end of it.

"Can we go walk around?" I ask.

"Yeah. We still need to get you a few things."

It feels good to get up and move around, and I tell myself that I can do an extra workout when I get home, and before the sun sets tonight, I will have burned off these calories. I am determined.

"Aren't you glad that you ate a good lunch?" she asks over the door to the dressing room, as I'm trying on a great-looking pair of jeans. "Don't you feel better?"

I nod as I zip the jeans, pleased that a size 9 fits perfectly and that my stomach does not look like a watermelon. This is the thinnest I have ever been! And, okay, I'm not a size 1 like Leah, I think as I examine these jeans from all angles, but I'm not half-bad either. I step out of the dressing room to show Leah now, and she claps her hands in approval.

"Those are perfect, Em. And see the way those pockets make your rearend look smaller?"

I turn and look again. But even as I'm looking, I'm thinking, yeah, she's right, that part of my body still needs some serious reduction. I'm not done losing weight yet. I mean, if I could drop four sizes, why not a couple more? Or at least I might be able to fit into a pair of size 7s by the time school starts in three weeks. Size 7s!

fifteen

"Looks like your back-to-school shopping was a success," my mom says when I come home buried beneath bags of clothes.

"Yeah," I tell her. "I can't believe I can actually wear a size 9 now. And some of the tops I got were smalls!" I open a bag and pull out a T-shirt just to show her.

She smiles, but it doesn't hide a look of concern in her eyes. "Are you going to stop dieting now?"

Dieting is what I've told my parents I'm doing. And I pretend to eat things like cereal in the morning, although I just dump it down the sink when no one's looking. Then, of course, I'm not home for lunch. And I usually just pick at a salad for dinner. My dad thinks I'm "doing great and exhibiting lots of willpower" when I pass up desserts and snacks. He seems oblivious to the fact that my weight loss has occurred relatively quickly. But Mom, on the other hand, continues to question me. We've even had a few fights over it. And the last time she complained, I told her that her pestering me would only make things worse. I think that helped some, because she's really let up. Until today.

"Emily," she persists, "I'm worried about your eating habits. I think it's time to stop this dieting and to start eating in a more healthy way."

I study her for a few seconds, standing there in her baggy old-lady jeans that she has to get in the plus-size section, and her dark-green tunic top, which is meant to camouflage her weight but looks more like an army tent that's gone soft. "I'm fine, Mom," I say. "Don't worry about the way I eat."

"But you don't eat," she says. "Do you?"

"What do you mean?"

"I mean, I saw Ronda the other day. She mentioned how you skip lunch in order to exercise by walking every day."

"What?" I demand. "Do you have spies now?"

"No, we were just talking. Ronda's the one who brought it up."

"Well, she might be my boss at work, but she's not the boss of my personal life. Ronda should mind her own business."

"She was concerned about you, honey."

"She should be concerned about herself, Mom. Have you noticed how heavy she is?"

Mom looks hurt now. And I realize that Ronda is probably smaller than Mom. "Ronda thinks you may have anorexia, Emily. And apparently she's not the only one. There's a girl who works in the coffee shop who has the same—"

"Frieda?" I spit out. "It just figures." I don't add that Frieda is fat too. It's like all the fat people are ganging up on me.

"Do you think it's possible?"

"What?" I'm so mad at Frieda and Ronda now that I can't even remember what we were talking about.

"Anorexia? Do you think you might have an eating disorder? I've been reading up on it, and it's really frightening, Emily. It can do damage to your body, and it really strains your heart when you over—"

"I'm not anorexic!" I practically scream at her, tossing my bags to the floor for effect.

"Hey," says Dad as he comes in from the garage, "what's the problem?"

"Mom's the problem," I say to him. "Just because I've been dieting and losing weight, she's all freaked that I'm anorexic."

Dad smiles at me now, looking at me with what feels like real approval, like I finally look like the daughter he's been wanting all these years. Then he turns to Mom, and I think I can see a slight frown creasing his brow. "Oh, I'm sure she's not anorexic, sweetheart. She's just been eating less and exercising more. Just like I'd been telling her to do. And it's working." He turns back and pats me on the back. "Keep up the good work, Emily. You're looking great."

Now I give Mom a victorious smile. "See," I tell her. "I'm fine. Just ask Dad."

However, she doesn't look convinced. And as I gather up my bags, I can't help but notice that her eyes are moist. She turns away to face the sink. I don't stick around to see her cry. And I don't blame myself for her sadness either. She's been like this a lot lately. I figure it's either menopause or the fact that she's getting sick and tired of being fat. I know I was. But, I tell myself, this isn't about me.

As I put my new clothes away, I am feeling seriously irked at Ronda and Frieda. What right do they have to go around talking about me? They're probably just jealous and trying to get back at me. I'm tempted to call the bookstore right now and tell Ronda that I quit. That would teach her. This is a busy time of year for the bookstore, and I'm a hard worker. I'm sure she'd be sorry that she interfered in my personal life.

"Emily?" calls my mom as she knocks on my door.

"What?" I say in a cranky voice, preparing myself for a whole new assault from her. Maybe she's come with food again. She's tried that quite a few times.

I open the door with a frown, ready to say, "No thanks!" to whatever sugary, fatty offering she might be hoping to tempt me with. But all she has in her hand is the phone. "It's for you."

Wondering why the person didn't call my cell phone, I answer it and am surprised to find that it's Pastor Ray. I also feel a little guilty—for a couple of reasons. First of all for skipping out on youth group this summer, and perhaps even more than that, I feel bad that I've been treating my mom so poorly this evening.

"Hi, Emily," he says. "How are you doing?"

"Okay," I tell him. "Just busy. I've been working at the bookstore, then helping Leah after her surgery and stuff." Right, make yourself sound good to the youth pastor. What a hypocrite I've turned into.

"Good to hear. I hope Leah's recovering."

"She is. I was just with her today. She's lots better."

"Oh, good. Well, I'm calling to ask you for a huge favor, Emily."

"What's that?" Pastor Ray wants a favor from me? What's wrong with this picture?

"I'm in charge of another camp during the last two weeks of August, and one of my worship leaders just bailed on me, and I remembered how great you were at filling in this past June. I just wondered if you might possibly be available to join the worship team."

"You want me to be a worship leader?"

"Yeah, it should be lots easier than being a cabin counselor, Emily. I know you had a rough time in June. This might actually feel like a vacation, since all you would do is help to lead singing before meals and then at campfire. The pay's not much, but—"

"It sounds great," I tell him.

"I was hoping you'd think so. I mean, we might've been okay with just three musicians, but God really put you on my heart. I just get this deep sense that God wants you there for those two weeks. I think he can really use you, Emily."

"But I do have my job at the bookstore."

"I'm sure that Ronda would let you go," he says quickly. Of course, Ronda goes to our church too—for all I know she and Pastor Ray could be in cahoots. Although I doubt it. "Especially if she realized that you were leaving to help out at camp. Maybe I could even talk to her for you."

"No . . ." The last thing I need is for Ronda to open her big mouth to Pastor Ray right now. "No, it's okay, I can talk to her. And at least I can give her a week's notice." Of course, I don't tell him how I was just imagining quitting on her today with no notice.

"That'd be great, Emily." Then he fills me in on some details, which go in one ear and out the other, and I promise to get back to him after I speak to Ronda.

Do I feel like a hypocrite when I hang up? Well, duh. I mean pretty much everything I've been doing lately seems a bit questionable, if not downright dishonest. But I remind myself of how Pastor Ray said that God had put me on his heart and how he believed God wanted me at this camp. And, okay, who am I to argue with God?

"What did Pastor Ray want?" Mom asks as I return the phone to the cradle in the kitchen downstairs.

I tell her about camp, hoping this will provide a good distraction for her—something to take her mind off of my so-called "eating disorder."

"Oh, that would be nice," she says as she washes a head of lettuce. "You're so good with your guitar and singing, Emily. I've often wondered why you don't do more with it."

"Really?" I study her. "Why didn't you ever tell me that?"

She shrugs. "I don't know. I suppose I just assumed that you knew how good you were."

"It doesn't hurt to hear that from others."

She turns and smiles at me. "You're right, Emily. I should've told you that a long time ago." Then she frowns, and I can tell she's thinking about my weight again. "But do you think you'll be okay at camp?"

"Why not?"

"You won't keep *dieting*, will you? Because you'll need your strength. Can you at least promise me that you'll eat while you're there?"

I glance away. I may be a hypocrite, but I hate lying to my mother.

"Emily?"

"I'll do my best, Mom."

Now she comes over, and I can tell she wants to hug me. And I don't fight it. I have to admit there is something very comforting about her softness, just enveloping me like that.

But then she steps back and just shakes her head. "You are too thin, Emily. If you don't stop this dieting, or whatever you want to call it, you'll be nothing but skin and bones."

I force a laugh. "I don't think so, Mom."

"I mean it, Emily. You need to take care of yourself. You're just wasting away."

"I don't see how you can say that," I tell her. "I wear a size 9 and Leah is about three sizes smaller. Do you think she's wasting away?"

She considers this. "Maybe so. Maybe the two of you are both anorexic."

"Oh, Mom." I roll my eyes.

Now she holds a carrot out for me. "Well, you can at least eat this, can't you?"

I take the carrot from her and take a bite. "Feel better now?" I say with my mouth full.

"Not much."

"Whatever," I say as I turn away with the carrot still in my hand. "I'm taking a walk." But as soon as I'm out of sight of the house, I ditch the carrot. I'm not stupid. I know that carrots are full of sugar. And I remember that lunch Leah forced me to eat today and all those calories I have to burn off before sunset. And I walk faster than ever.

***

As it turns out, Ronda has no problem with my quitting before summer ends. She almost seems relieved.

"You're a good worker," she tells me on my last day. She's asked me to come back to her office to pick up my check. "But I'd be lying to say that I'm not worried about you, Emily."

"Thanks." I say as I stick the envelope into my purse. I don't want to do anything to encourage this conversation.

"I know that you have an eating disorder."

I look toward the door, wondering how rude it would be to just make a run for it. Take the money and run.

"And I suspect that you're anorexic."

Now I look directly at her, still not answering, but hoping that my stare will somehow threaten her—like how dare she attack me about my weight when she has a weight problem herself?

"I know what you think, Emily. You're probably thinking, *Why should this fat woman have an opinion about me or my body?*"

I kind of shrug, like yeah.

"Well, let me tell you a little story. Believe it or not, I used to be a lot like you. I was a little overweight as a teen, and I decided to do something about it. I tried a bunch of diets, and finally, in desperation, I just quit eating. And, like you, I became anorexic. I remember the thrill of not eating, of losing weight, and the powerful way I felt when I exercised to excess."

I'm sure I look pretty skeptical now. Like, yeah, you bet.

"I kept it up for a couple of years too. I finally got so sick that my parents intervened and made me get help. And it took a long time, but finally I got over it." She kind of laughs now. "Obviously, I got over it really well."

"And?" I let out a sigh of exasperation.

"And I completely ruined my metabolism, Emily. Two years of starving myself taught my body how to survive on practically nothing. And now I can diet until the cows come home and not lose an ounce. I swear if I were ever in a starvation camp, I'd be the last one standing."

For some reason this gets my attention. Still, I don't respond.

"But there might still be hope for you, Emily. How long have you been doing this anyway?"

I consider this. "About three months, I guess."

"Tell me something," she says, pausing for a moment, probably to just draw me in. "Does it make you happy?"

I consider this. Happy? I can't remember the last time I was really happy, but I know it would've been before I began this whole diet thing. Still, I just shrug.

"I didn't think so. I mean, we think being thin will make us happy, but it never does."

"Neither does being fat."

"Maybe not. But at least it doesn't kill you. I mean, if you don't let your weight get out of control. Not like anorexia. It always gets out of control. You think you're in control, Emily, but you're not. You have to get control over the anorexia. If you don't get control over it, it's going to control you—maybe forever. Sure, you might be able to stay skinny. I have a friend who's done that. But you should see her. She's forty, never been married, never had kids. She's nothing but skin and bones and has lots and lots of serious health issues. Even her hair is falling out. But she is still ruled by anorexia—it dominates every single choice she makes. She literally has no life. Really, I can take you to see her if you don't believe me. Or you could end up like me, fighting a metabolism that could put a snail to shame. Take your pick. But that's the long-term prognosis for anorexics—if they survive. Some don't."

Despite my attempts to shut out her comments, they're getting to me. What she's saying actually makes some sense. "But what do I do?" I ask her. "How do I stop this when I still want to be thin? When I still want to lose more weight?"

"First of all, you need to realize and admit that it's wrong. And you need to accept the fact that you've fallen into the trap."

"Trap?"

"Of believing you still need to lose weight. Because, trust me, you could never lose enough. Once you start seeing yourself like this, it's like looking in one of those fun-house mirrors where the image is all stretched out and distorted. You see fat no matter what you weigh. It never ends. So you have to accept that your thinking, as far as weight is concerned, has become skewed."

"How do you get unskewed?"

She kind of laughs. "Well, there are treatments, of course. And I can give you some names." She grabs a notepad from her desk and starts to write while she talks. "You might also want to check out some of these websites. It's a good way to get information without actually walking in for an appointment. Something they didn't have back when I was your age."

I nod like I might do that, although I doubt that I will.

"But I have to say," she continues, handing me her quickly scrawled list, "the thing that helped me the most was God. I honestly could not have escaped my anorexia without him. I just wish I would've done it a lot sooner. Like after only three months." She holds her hands out. "Then maybe I wouldn't look like this."

Her hint doesn't escape me, but I still feel hopeless.

"I decided to give my eating habits to God. I told him that my body wasn't mine, but his, and that I wanted him to help me make wise choices. It didn't happen overnight, and like I said, my parents did a pretty dramatic intervention thing with me. But it wasn't until I actually made the choice—inviting God to help me—that things actually began to change." She finally stops talking and just looks at me.

"Thanks," I tell her, unsure as to whether her words will change anything for me or not. But I do get what she's saying. I really do.

"Sorry to butt in like that. But when you've been there, done that . . . well, it's hard to just stand by and watch someone else make the same mistakes."

"Yeah. I can understand that."

"I'll be praying for you, Emily."

"Thanks."

"Have a good time at camp." She gets a big grin now. "I hear you're hot stuff on the guitar."

I kind of shrug. "I'm okay, I guess." Of course, I don't tell her I've been practicing like mad all week long. I'd neglected playing as much as I used to, using that time to exercise more. It's like you have to choose. But all this week, I've been practicing like my life depended on it. Not that I can explain this yet, but I have a sense that maybe it does.

As I walk home, I think about what Ronda just told me. Part of me thinks she's telling the truth, but another part of me says she's just jealous and that she wishes she weren't so fat. Consequently, she wants to mess with my mind so that I'll end up like her. And while I can see that the first part makes more sense, is more believable, and probably right, the other part has such a strong pull that by the time I get home, I'm just not sure anymore.

sixteen

As I'm packing for camp on Sunday night, I can't help but notice the difference between the clothes I'm taking this time compared to what I took only two months ago. I hold up my faithful old Gap shorts that used to be too tight and actually consider taking them with me, but then I remember how Leah said they look pathetic, and I have to admit they do kind of hang on me now. But it's still sort of fun to see them all loose and baggy. Kind of amazing, really.

I stand before my full-length mirror, carefully checking out these surprisingly roomy shorts as I try to decide whether or not they can survive two more weeks of hard wear. But I have to admit that Leah is probably right. Besides being too big, the faded denim has worn pretty thin, and these shorts really do look a little worse for wear. And that's when I notice my own pale image in the mirror. I can't help but think, like my shorts, I'm looking a little faded and worse for wear. Or maybe I'm just tired. I remember how Pastor Ray said these next two weeks of camp will feel almost like a vacation—I just hope he's right.

As I'm getting some stuff from the bathroom, it occurs to me that I should take a box of tampons along, and then it hits me that my period is actually late. And not just a few days either. When I actually check the calendar, I discover that it's more than two weeks late. Now if I were the kind of girl to mess around, I might *really* be worried. As it is, I am still somewhat worried. And there's this nagging impression that it might have something to do with my diet and exercise regime.

I've been trying not to think too hard about what Ronda said. I guess I still question her motives. Or maybe that's just my excuse to dismiss her "advice." But then I remember her challenge for me to go online and check out the anorexia websites she wrote down. And I have a feeling these particular spots are put together by medical professionals, not just more anorexic girls giving their get-thin-quick tips to people like me.

So, even though it's late, I decide to do some quick research. Mostly to see if this missing-period thing might be related. That might put my mind at ease. And, besides, who cares about not having a period once in a while? No biggie.

But instead of relief, all I get is more anxiety. The more I see, and the more I read, the scarier this whole anorexia thing gets. The list of all the side effects that can arise from eating disorders is pretty freaky. Here are the "complications" I read from just one list. Certain things seem to stand out to me.

- Irregular heartbeat, cardiac arrest, **<u>death</u>**
- Kidney damage, **<u>death</u>**
- Liver damage, **<u>death</u>**
- Esophagus rupture, teeth erosion, loss of muscle and bone mass
- Stomach ulcers, gastritis, gastric distress
- **<u>Disruption of menstrual cycle</u>**, eventual infertility
- Delayed growth and stunted growth
- Immune-system deficiency
- Blood-circulation problems, resulting in cold hands and feet

- Swollen glands and salivary duct stones, resulting in "chipmunk cheeks"
- Excess hair growth on face and body
- Dry, blotchy complexion with gray or yellow tones
- Anemia, life-threatening fluid and mineral imbalances, **death**
- Seizures, fainting, sleep disorders, hallucinations, fuzzy thinking
- Low blood sugar that leads to tremors, anxiety, restlessness, and an uncontrollable itchy feeling
- Osteoporosis and bone fractures
- Anal and bladder incontinence
- Urinary tract, vaginal, and kidney infections
- Chronic constipation
- Low estrogen levels, leading to atrophy of pelvic floor muscles, which must be surgically repaired

Okay, I'm thinking the lesser problems—like having yellow or blotchy skin, facial hair, "chipmunk cheeks," cold hands and feet, and constipation—are bad enough in and of themselves, and I've even experienced a few of those already. But I see now that those are relatively minor compared to some of the other stuff on that list. It's hard to lightly dismiss things like permanent kidney and liver damage, heart problems, and, well, *death*. This website makes anorexia nervosa seem quite serious.

Amazingly, there's a part of me that wants to tune all this out, to just toss this information aside and pretend like it's nothing more than propaganda created to frighten anorexics into behaving like "normal" people, fat people.

Even so, I have this uncontrollable urge to keep reading and rereading this list, like I want to imprint it into my brain, like maybe this frightening information will help me to get out of this mess somehow. But when I finally turn off my computer, the words just slip away, like I can't even remember them. Well, maybe except for the part about fuzzy thinking. I guess that's how I feel. Like my brain is tired. Maybe I'm just ready to hit the hay.

But when I go to bed, I'm restless and unable to sleep. Wasn't restlessness one of the complications? I tell myself I'm just wired about camp, too excited to sleep. But as the night wears on, and the clock now says it's 3:17 and I'm still wide awake, I'm not so sure anymore.

My body feels like I've just run a mile. My heart is racing and jumping—like it's going to pop right out of my chest. And yet I'm not even moving. I put my hand on my chest and try to count the beats and see how many there are per minute, but the beats are irregular. Some are strong and some are weak, and I'm not sure which ones to count. And soon I lose track and tell myself to forget about it. Even so, something doesn't feel right.

I try to tell myself that I'm simply overreacting to what I read earlier tonight, that I'm acting like a hypochondriac and that these feelings are psychosomatic, and that if I just concentrate on something else, these feelings will go away. So I breathe deeply and slowly, and then I make myself count from one hundred backward. But when I'm done I feel even worse. My heart is still pounding way too hard and way too irregularly. I think I'm starting to panic.

I get out of bed and begin to pace around my room, trying to see if this activity helps or makes things worse. Then I go to the bathroom and slowly drink a glass of water. But nothing seems to change anything, and by 4:00 a.m., I think I could really be having an honest-to-goodness heart attack. So I walk down the hall to my parents' room and stand there for a couple of minutes, considering whether to knock on their door and tell them what's up.

The idea of waking my parents in the middle of the night to tell them I think I'm having a heart attack is so bizarre. And I know my mom would freak and immediately call 9-1-1, and then what will happen to me? I'll probably be dragged off in an ambulance, and then at the hospital they will inform me that I'm perfectly fine and that this whole thing was just my imagination. How embarrassing would that be? I walk back to my room, telling myself to just chill.

Then I think maybe I should force myself to eat something. Maybe I'm having one of those low-blood-sugar symptoms I read about. So I go down to the kitchen and look around. I see calorie-laden things like cookies and chips and I just cringe. How can I eat something like that? I open the fridge and everything in there seems to be leering at me, and it reminds me of that scene in *Alice in Wonderland*, only instead of pills it's the food that says, "Eat me and you will get very big." I slam the door shut and just lean into the breakfast bar, my heart pounding harder than ever now. Maybe I will die right here, in the kitchen, right in front of the refrigerator. The coroner's report will probably say that I starved myself to death. But I really don't want to die. I'm too young to die.

"God, help me," I pray as I cling to the tiled surface. "Please, please, help me, dear God. I know that something is wrong with me, and it's probably all my fault for the way I've been treating my body. I've been stupid, God. I'm sorry. Please, help me, God. I want to change. I'll do my best. I don't want to die."

And I continue praying like that, half standing, half sprawled across the breakfast bar, begging God to keep me from dying. Being alone in the middle of the night and feeling the way I do, dying feels like a real possibility.

Finally, it's about five, and I am feeling a little calmer. And to my utter amazement, I am able to take a banana out of the fruit bowl and, knowing full well that bananas are packed full of carb calories, simply peel it and then slowly eat it. One tiny bite at a time. Then I pour myself a half glass of two-percent milk, and I slowly drink it without really considering that it's not skim. Then, even though the sun is coming up, I go back to bed. And I sleep until eight thirty, which means I have exactly fifteen minutes to get to the church parking lot, which is thirty minutes away.

"Are you feeling okay?" Mom asks as she drives me to church, going as fast as the speed limits will allow.

"Yeah," I tell her as I pull a brush through my hair. "I just didn't sleep very good last night. But I got up and ate a banana and had some milk, and then I felt better."

Mom smiles with what I'm sure is relief. "Oh, good for you, honey. That's probably just what you needed."

"Yeah, maybe." I'm attempting to put on some mascara and lip gloss with the aid of the vibrating sun-visor mirror, all the while hoping that I haven't been left behind. I'd feel really bad to let Pastor Ray down.

There's only one van left in the parking lot when we get to the church, waiting for me, it turns out. I tell Mom a hasty good-bye, then rush over to the van and apologize for being late. Fortunately for me, the driver, my old Sunday-school teacher Mrs. Adams, is understanding and patient.

"No problem, Emily," she tells me, indicating that I should sit in the seat beside her. "Pastor Ray said you'd be coming and to wait."

I glance in the back of the van to see three younger girls and a girl about my age, who I assume is a counselor. She's helping with the blonde girl's seat belt, and I'm not sure why, but for some reason I get the impression that these kids aren't exactly "normal." But, of course, I don't say anything. Maybe this is the handicapped van, and that's why we were last to leave. Whatever. I don't really care. I'm just glad they waited for me.

I tell Mrs. Adams about not getting much sleep last night and how that's what made me late, and she tells me to just lean back and take a nap if I'd like. And so I do.

When I wake up, we're already in the camp parking lot, and the counselor, whose name I've now heard is Melissa, is helping a girl named Gina into a wheelchair. And as I get out of the van, I notice other kids and counselors milling about the parking lot, and I realize that all the kids here, at least all the ones I can see, appear to have some kind of disability.

As I help Mrs. Adams unload some bags and supplies, I quietly ask her about this camp. "I kind of got drafted at the last minute," I say, "so I wasn't really sure what the age group was and stuff . . ."

She smiles at me. "The last camp of the year is always for special-needs campers ages eight to eighteen."

I nod as if this is the most normal thing in the world. "Cool," I say. But what I'm actually thinking is, this looks like some kind of freak show. Okay, I hate admitting that, and it just shows how shallow I really am. But as I look around at all these kids with all these problems, well, I start feeling pretty depressed. It is just so sad, and I wish I hadn't agreed to come.

"Hey," says Pastor Ray. "You made it."

I explain to him about not sleeping and how it made me late. "I felt kind of sick last night," I finally say.

He frowns. "But you're okay now?"

"Yeah. I feel better. Just kinda tired."

"Well, the worship team plans to meet at eleven to do some practicing. You might be able to grab a quick nap until then." He tells me where my room is, a private one up in the lodge.

"Just like a VIP," I say.

He nods. "Yep. Enjoy."

So I take my guitar case and duffel bag and sleeping bag and go off in search of my private room. And I have to admit that I feel relieved to get away from these kids with their oxygen tanks and wheelchairs and other kinds of medical paraphernalia. This whole scene kind of gives me the heebie-jeebies.

I'm in room number 12, and although it's small and nothing fancy, I am so glad that I don't have to share it with anyone else. I unpack a few things, noticing as I do that Mom must've sneaked some snacks into my duffel bag. And I'm just about to toss these offensive items into the trash when I stop myself. I remember how sick I felt last night, and how I prayed to God, begging him to help me, and how I promised him that I'd start doing things differently, and that I'd start taking care of myself and eating right.

So I set the blueberry muffin, the banana and apple, and the package of string cheese on the little dresser right next to my bed, and then I lie down, promising myself that I will eat something when I wake up in about an hour.

seventeen

IT'S NEARLY ELEVEN WHEN I WAKE FROM MY NAP. I'M TOTALLY DISORIENTED AND practically run into the wall when I climb out of bed. The remnants of a bad dream are still hanging on to me—I'd been trying to run from a bunch of dismembered people, and they wanted to catch me so they could cut off my arms and legs to use for themselves. Really creepy.

It's just because of the special-needs kids, I tell myself as I do a quick check in the mirror and grab my guitar case. Get over it. Then I see the food on the little dresser and remember that I haven't eaten. I reach for the apple and then draw back, almost as if the apple is poisoned. Then I go for the cheese and almost touch it, but it's like there's another force at work here, like some other kind of power that's controlling me.

"Come on," I tell myself. "Just pick it up and eat it."

But it's like I'm standing here, fighting this crazy little battle. And it feels like I am losing, like I absolutely have no strength. Finally, I decide to just take the apple. I put it in my sweatshirt pocket, promising myself that I will eat it on the way to the mess hall, the place where we're supposed to practice.

Just pull out the apple and take a bite as you walk, I command myself. But I just cannot do it. Instead I tell myself that I will eat

161

something at lunch, and that it's only an hour and a half away, and that it won't hurt me a bit to wait. But even as I say this to myself, I have a strong sense that I am lying, that I'm deceiving myself, and that I'm thinking I can deceive God as well. I basically make myself sick.

Finally, I'm just outside of the mess hall, and I stop and tell myself that I cannot go in unless I eat at least three bites from that stupid apple. Just do it!

So I set down my guitar case, remove the apple, and take one tentative bite, slowly chewing until it's turned to liquid, and then I will myself to swallow. Why is this so freaking hard? I glance through the window to see that a couple of other people are already inside, appearing to be tweaking the sound system. And, according to the big clock in there, it's nearly eleven. I force myself to swallow.

Only two more bites, I tell myself. The second one is nearly as hard as the first, although I notice the third one's a bit easier. And finally I am done. I have reached my goal, and I can go inside. I toss the remainder of the apple in the trash barrel by the door, then open the door. Okay, I realize that's not much to eat, but I think it's a start and better than nothing.

"Hey, Emily," calls a familiar voice. And I look over to where a guy with a guitar case is just coming in the side door.

"Brett!" I say, feeling excitement for the first time since I arrived. "What are you doing here?"

"I'm on the worship team too. I just heard a few days ago that you're joining us. Welcome!"

"Thanks. It's cool to be here. Pastor Ray just asked me to come last week. I had to quit my job and everything."

"It'll be worth it. These next two weeks are going to be awesome. This is the coolest camp of the summer."

I nod, wishing I shared his genuine enthusiasm. "I can't wait."

"Well then, let's not wait," calls a short red-headed guy from up front. "Let's get started, guys."

He begins by introducing himself to the rest of us. "I'm Harris Myers," he says, "and I'm in charge of the worship team. I'm a senior in college, my major is music, and I play several different instruments, but the most important thing I can tell you is that my heart belongs to Jesus. Next?" He points to Brett.

"I'm Brett McEwen, and I'm going to be a senior in high school. I play electric and acoustic guitar and bass and drums, and I'm just learning banjo. And, oh yeah, I'm sold out to the Lord too."

"Cool," says Harris. "Maybe I can give you some banjo tips." Then he turns to the heavy-set guy who's sitting in front of the keyboard.

"I'm Nick," says the guy in a shy voice. "I'm a friend of Harris', and I play keyboards and drums, and I've only been a Christian for about a year."

"Don't let his humble introduction fool you," says Harris. "Nick's not only a really gifted musician, but he's got a great heart and his relationship with the Lord is rock solid. Right, Nick?"

He kind of nods.

"And our worship-leader chick." Harris smiles at me now.

"I'm Emily Foster," I begin, wishing I'd taken time to think of something halfway cool to say, "and I play acoustic guitar. And I gave my heart to the Lord when I was about eleven."

Harris nods. "Cool. How about if we ask God to knit our hearts and our music together in a way that totally glorifies him during the next two weeks?"

And so we do. The prayers seem really genuine and I feel my spirits lifting, and I'm thinking maybe this is exactly where I need to be during the next two weeks. Practice even goes pretty well, although I mess up a couple of times and feel like I'm having a hard time focusing. Afterward, I apologize to the guys. "It's probably just nerves," I tell them. "But, don't worry, I'll be practicing in my free time."

Fortunately, I do better when we play for the kids as they're coming in for lunch. And I think we actually sound pretty good together, although I know that I have lots of room for improvement. And after everyone gets seated, which takes a lot longer than it did at the last camp, I notice that there are a lot more counselors, like almost a one-to-one ratio, but I suspect this is because these kids need lots of help just getting around. Pastor Ray comes up and welcomes everyone to camp, then asks a blessing for the lunch. Then, as the servers come with the food, Pastor Ray introduces the members of the worship team, and we play a couple more songs. At the end of each song, the reaction from the campers is pretty awesome. They clap like they really mean it.

"Time to eat," says Harris after he's turned off the mike. "The worship team's table is right over there."

So I take my time putting my guitar back into its case, telling myself that I will eat and behave like a normal person, then I go over and join the guys.

"The food here's not half-bad for camp food," says Brett as he passes Nick the bowl of spaghetti.

I go for the green salad, since it's right in front of me. And while I take a fairly generous portion, I do leave room on my plate for other things.

"Dressing?" says Harris as he passes the container to me.

"Thanks." My arm feels like lead as I pour some of the thick, white ranch dressing onto my salad. I can do this, I'm telling myself.

Soon I have salad, spaghetti, and garlic bread on my plate. And I feel certain that I'll never be able to eat all of it, probably not even half of it. Each bite takes an act of will, and each swallow feels like a total betrayal to my body. I imagine the pounds piling back on, obliterating all that I have worked so hard for.

"Not hungry?" asks Brett when he notices that I still have a lot of food on my plate. The three guys are nearly done.

I shrug. "I had kind of an upset stomach this morning," I tell him. This isn't entirely untrue, since I was practically having a heart attack.

"Nerves," says Harris. "I used to get like that all the time before a performance. My stomach would tie itself in knots. Sometimes I even lost my lunch before I'd go on stage."

Nick nods. "Yeah. I was the same. In fact, I still feel like that sometimes. Don't worry, Emily. It'll get better in time."

"Thanks." I pretend to nibble at the garlic bread. Having these guys excusing my light eating seems to give me permission to eat less. And when the server comes to clear our table, I don't stop her from taking my plate.

"You've lost a lot of weight, haven't you?" Brett's looking at me with a slight frown. "I mean since June."

"Yeah. I've been on a diet this summer."

"You girls and your diets," says Harris. "I think chicks take the whole skinny thing way too far. Give me a girl with meat on her bones over a skinny one any day."

This makes the other guys laugh. But I'm seriously thinking about what he just said. Did he really mean that, or was he just trying to make me feel better about myself? My dilemma is that although Harris seems like a nice guy, I can't imagine he really cares how I feel about myself. I mean, he doesn't even know me. So maybe he is telling the truth.

"Time for more music," says Harris. We follow him back to where our stuff is set up, pick up our instruments, and begin to play. I feel myself relaxing, and I can tell I'm playing better. But when I look out at the kids who are just finishing their lunches, I notice how one girl has no arms and her counselor is helping her to eat, even wiping a piece of spaghetti from her chin. And there's a boy whose body is so twisted that his head is nearly in his lap, but I can see him smiling as he listens to our music. It makes me want to cry.

We play for about ten minutes. Once again, when we stop, the kids clap and cheer. Some even yell out for more.

"There's lots more," Harris assures them. "We're going to be playing at all the meals and at campfire, and by the time these two weeks are over, you'll be sick of us!"

This makes them laugh, and some protest that they won't be sick of us. And then, feeling a little like rock stars, we exit out the back.

"Good job, guys," says Harris when we're outside. "But let's plan another practice for, say, three o'clock. My plan is to practice several times during the first few days, just so we get comfortable with each other and make sure we know the songs and arrangements and stuff. After that, we'll just see how it goes. I realize you guys aren't getting paid much more than slave wages for this, and I don't want to work you to the bone."

"Sounds great to me," says Brett. "I plan to be helping out a little at the lake in my spare time."

"Cool," says Harris. "I said I'd be on hand at the pool."

"I'm gonna hang out at the craft shop," says Nick.

Then they all look at me. I kind of shrug. "I'm not sure what I'll be doing."

"You mean Pastor Ray didn't rope you into helping yet?" asks Brett.

I shake my head. "I'm kinda the latecomer, remember."

"Well, watch out," he warns with a smile. "He'll be coming after you."

"Just don't let him talk you into archery," says Harris. "I heard a counselor actually took an arrow to the behind at special camp last year."

"Thanks for the advice."

"And if Pastor Ray doesn't hit you up for help," says Brett, "you can always come down to the lake and give me a hand."

"I'll keep that in mind," I tell him. Then, not really knowing what to do with myself, or even what I want to do, I head for my room. As I walk past the girls' restroom, I have to fight this really strong urge to go in there and gag myself. Everything in me wants to get rid of what little lunch I forced myself to consume. And then I want to go outside and exercise. I want to walk until I'm sweating and hot and exhausted. Or maybe I could swim laps. Or hike up to the waterfall. Anything to burn fat.

"No," I say out loud as I close the door to my room. "That's not going to happen this time." But then I just stand there in total frustration. I feel like screaming and crying and breaking things. It's like I'm being torn, like I'm trapped in one of those old torture chambers where they put someone on the rack and pull in opposite directions until the person is dismembered. How could I let go of everything I've worked so hard for during these past few months? How could I let myself get fat again? Maybe I *would* rather be dead. This is too hard.

Then I go and look in the mirror. It's only big enough to show my reflection from the waist up, and I'm certain that I'll see a bulge in what has otherwise become a fairly flat stomach as a result of all the sit-ups I do, both in the morning and at night. I pull up my shirt and examine my midsection from every possible angle and don't think I see too much change—not yet anyway. Although I do see that I'm still overweight and that I could still afford to take off a few pounds. Like maybe ten.

And then I remember what Ronda said about how it's never enough, no matter how much weight you lose, it's never enough. How could you be nothing but skin and bones and still believe that you're too fat? And to be honest, I do remember girls like that in Chicago, back when Leah and I went to modeling school. I also remember thinking I'd never be like that. I felt certain that I'd never fall into those traps. And yet here I am, a prisoner. What is the difference between them and me?

Feeling desperate and scared and hopeless, and almost certain that I'll never be able to escape my self-made trap and that I'm in over my head, I pull out my cell phone and speed-dial Leah's number, praying that she'll pick up.

"Hey, Emily," she says in a calm voice. "I was just thinking about you. How's it going?"

"I need to talk." I feel like it's hard to breathe, like I just got done running. "Are you busy right now?"

"Nope. Go ahead."

So I pour it all out. I tell her how I thought I was actually dying last night, how I promised God that I'd start eating right again, and how I really meant it when I said it, but how it all feels totally impossible to me now.

"I mean, I really do want to get healthy again." I sigh loudly. "But I just don't know if I can actually do it, you know? It's like I feel trapped. Like I've started this thing and I don't know how to stop it."

"This is exactly like what I was reading in the Bible just this morning!"

"Huh?"

"Here, let me read it to you. Do you mind?"

"I guess not."

"Okay. I want you to sit down and just listen to this. I'm reading from *The Message*, the same as your Bible—you took your Bible with you, right?"

"Yeah. It's here somewhere."

"Okay, this is from Ephesians, chapter six, verses eleven to thirteen. Here goes: 'So take everything the Master has set out for you, well-made weapons of the best materials. And put them to use so you will be able to stand up to everything the Devil throws your way. This is no afternoon athletic contest that we'll walk away from and forget about in a couple of hours. This is for keeps, a life-or-death fight to the finish against the Devil and all his angels. Be prepared. You're up against far more than you can handle on your own. Take all the help you can get, every weapon God has issued, so that when it's all over but the shouting you'll still be on your feet.' Isn't that totally awesome, Emily?"

"Yeah, I guess. I mean, I've heard it before . . ."

"Listen to this part again, okay? 'This is for keeps, a life-or-death fight to the finish against the Devil and all his angels.' That's like what you're up against, Em. You're in this battle. Can't you feel it?"

"Yeah, as a matter of fact, I can. It does feel like a battle."

"And it's not just for your body, Emily. It's for your soul too. Because think about it, if you lose this battle over your body . . . well, then what happens to your soul?"

"I know . . . I know what you mean." I feel even more desperate now. "So what do I do? How do I fight this battle?"

"You need to be really praying, Em. And reading your Bible. And you may need to talk to someone at camp, someone who can be kind of a prayer warrior with you, you know what I mean? Someone you can talk to about this."

I immediately think of Brett and how we were prayer partners during the last camp. But how can I tell him about something like this—a stupid eating disorder? Anorexia? He'll think I'm nuts.

"Is there someone you can talk to?"

"Brett McEwen is here."

"Seriously?" She laughs. "You know I got the feeling that boy was into you last June, Em. You guys spent some time together."

"We were prayer partners," I say in exasperation. "He had a tough group of boys, and we made a commitment to pray for each other. That was all."

"Well, great. Ask him to partner with you again."

"I don't know . . ."

"Do you want to win this battle or not?"

I look at the snack foods that my mom sent, still sitting on the little dresser by my bed, lined up like soldiers. I can imagine them sitting there untouched for the entire two weeks until they are dried up and moldy and gross, and I will have lost the battle. "Yeah," I say, "I do want to win this battle."

"Then you need to be praying and reading your Bible, and I really think you need a prayer warrior to support you when the going is tough."

"But can't that be you?"

"Yeah, definitely. But I'm not there, Em. You need someone who's right there with you, someone who can see if you're doing what you need to or not, someone who will call you on it."

I let out a loud groan. "Why is this so hard?"

"Because the Devil doesn't want you to win, Emily! It's that simple. And especially when you're at a camp where you're supposed to minister to others with your music. He'd really like to destroy you. And if he destroys you, he can really mess things up for a lot of people at the same time. It becomes a win-win for the Devil and a lose-lose for you. Can't you see that?"

"Yeah," I admit, "I guess I can."

"So you'll take my advice then?"

I close my eyes and swallow hard. "Yes. I'll do my best."

"This is so exciting!"

"Uh-huh . . ."

"No, seriously. It's so cool that I was just reading that verse and praying for you and then you call. It's like God is really at work here. And you know why I think that is?"

"No, why?" I'm sure my voice sounds disinterested, but mostly I'm just overwhelmed.

"Because I'm finally putting my inner life above my exterior life. I'm letting God change me, and he's showing me how to live for him. And I'm finding out that it's pretty cool."

"How are your boobs?"

She laughs. "Oh, they're healing up. Slowly. But if I could turn back the clock and reverse that whole thing, I really would. That was so stupid."

I wonder if I would do the same. If I could turn the clock back to last May when I was forty pounds heavier and miserable, would I? The honest truth is that I don't think so. I really don't want to be fat again. And this scares me. Yet at the same time, I don't want to be anorexic either. The fact is, I want to have my cake and eat it too. I'm pathetic.

"This *is* a battle," I admit to Leah. "I just hope that I don't end up losing it."

"You won't, Em," she assures me. "Now write down these Bible verses, okay? And then read them and really take them into your heart. And pray. And don't forget to get a prayer partner."

So I write down the references to the verses and thank her, promising to keep her informed of my progress, or my lack thereof, which seems more likely. And then I take my Bible out of my duffel bag, and I actually sit down on my bed to look up the verses.

But after rereading the section that Leah already read to me on the phone, my eyelids feel so heavy and I feel so completely tired that I just end up falling asleep. Great start on the battle.

eighteen

W<small>HEN</small> I <small>WAKE UP</small>, I'<small>M HOT AND GROGGY AND, ONCE AGAIN, DISORIENTED.</small> Or maybe it's simply "fuzzy thinking"—just one of the many lovely side effects of anorexia nervosa. I see my Bible, still lying open on the bed, and I look at the Ephesians verses again, rereading the words aloud in the hope that the sound alone will pound them into my weary brain.

It's not three o'clock yet, too early to go practice, but I feel like I need some fresh air to clear my head. Also, my water bottle is empty and I am really, really thirsty. I notice the snacks my mom sent still sitting in a straight row on the dresser. And I feel an unexpected impulse to pick up the banana, but as usual, I hesitate. Talk about your high-carb fruits. Bananas are by far the worst. I stand there just staring at the stupid banana—like it's him against me. *Just eat it*, I tell myself. No biggie. Just pick it up and eat it.

"God, help me," I pray as I reach again for the banana. Then I pick it up, and without allowing myself to second-guess this choice, I begin to peel it and then take off a small bite, slowly chewing it, fighting back a gag reflex, and finally managing to swallow. Why is this so freaking hard?

I sit down on the bed again with the banana in one hand and the Bible in my lap. And as I slowly eat the banana, I read and reread the

Ephesians verses. And before I fully realize what's happened, I find that the banana is gone! All of it.

I look around the room, almost as if I expect to spy a little monkey hiding in the corner as he polishes off my banana. But there is no monkey. Only me. And I realize that I really did eat the whole thing, and my stomach doesn't even hurt.

Feeling somewhat victorious, I pick up my water bottle and my guitar. But then I feel a strong impulse to set down the water bottle and leave it behind. And yet I'm really thirsty.

Drink something that will nourish you.

Okay, I know I didn't actually hear those words, not audibly anyway, unless I really am going crazy, and I don't think I am. But I have this strong sense that I heard it on some level. And I have a strong sense that I should listen. So I set down my water bottle, shove some money into my shorts pocket, and head out to the Snack Shack, where I buy a bottle of apple juice and drink it. Then, because I'm still thirsty, I buy a bottle of SoBe green tea, knowing full well that it's sweetened, and not artificially. And I drink it.

By the time I go to practice, I'm feeling more energized than I have in weeks. I guess I'm partially jazzed over the idea that I'm somehow engaging in this spiritual war—and maybe even winning this particular battle, although I'm fully aware that this is only the beginning and I could easily lose the next. In fact, to be honest, I almost expect to lose the next.

Still, I tell myself, this could be a turning point. It's possible that I really can get out of my anorexic trap. But even as the hope of that hits me, I am hit by another thought, one that's more grim: *You may escape the anorexic trap, but you'll be fat again.* It makes me want to scream or cry or just give up. As I walk down the path, the phrase *fat, fat, fat—you must go back to that* is reverberating through my head in time with my steps.

"Hey, Em," says Brett as he jogs up and joins me as I walk toward the mess hall. "How's it going?"

"Okay." I try to erase that "fat" line from my head, and I force a wimpy smile at him.

"Feeling better?"

I nod. "Yeah. A little." But even as I say this, I can feel how false it is. Okay, maybe I did feel a little better for a second, but right now, I feel utterly hopeless. And I'm fighting the urge to run to the bathroom and barf. I'm also considering the idea of walking about ten miles after we finish practice, and then I'll eat dinner like a normal person, then head to the bathroom as soon as I'm done. This entire well-conceived plan flashes through my head in less than a second, I'm sure.

But then I remember Leah's challenge to me and how I promised to find a prayer partner, and I have an impression that this could be my opportunity. "Can I ask you a really big favor, Brett?"

"Sure. Shoot."

I consider how to begin. "This isn't easy . . ."

"Want to sit down a minute?" He stops by the bench in front of the mess hall, and we both sit down.

"Thanks." I take a deep breath, wondering how to say this—*just say it.* "I need to talk to someone. And I promised Leah that I would. She said I need a prayer-warrior partner."

"Hey, no problem. Remember, we did that during the last camp. But I know you don't have any crazy campers to deal with this time."

"No . . . just myself." I turn and look at him. "Can I trust you?"

He looks slightly uncomfortable but says, "Yeah."

"Okay, this is the deal. I got so obsessed with losing weight this summer that I actually became anorexic." I feel my cheeks burning with this admission. I can't believe I actually said it. And I have no idea how he'll react.

He nods. "Yeah, that's not too surprising."

I kind of blink. Did I hear him right? He's not surprised? Or maybe the reason he's not surprised is because he figures that's the only way a fat girl like me could lose that much weight so quickly. Whatever. I've taken this hard step, why not take another?

"Well, it kind of surprised me," I admit. "I never really meant for it to get like this. Not at the beginning. I just wanted to lose some weight before school started again. It didn't seem like a big deal."

"I can understand that. But the thing is, I've seen this happen before, Emily. My older sister, Audra, has really struggled with anorexia and bulimia. She's in her twenties now and still doesn't have it under control. So I guess I've gotten so I kinda recognize what it looks like, you know?"

"Seriously? Your sister?"

"Yeah. So I really do know how hard it is."

"Well, I've decided I want to stop." I feel tears now. They could be from relief or embarrassment or just plain desperation, but the last thing I want to do is to start crying in front of Brett. I mean, it's so cool that he gets this, that he understands. But what happens if I fall apart? *Please, please,* I warn myself, *don't blow this thing by bawling.*

"Good for you."

"But I can tell it's not going to be easy. I mean, it seems like every single bite is a great big battle." Then I tell him about the verses Leah read to me and how I am treating my anorexia like a real spiritual battle. "I just don't want to lose it," I finally say. "And Leah thinks that if someone here knows what's going on with me, well . . . that they can pray for me and check on me, you know, kinda like baby-sitting, I guess." I roll my eyes.

"Hey, I'm cool with that."

"Really?"

"Yeah. No problem. Just don't get mad at me if I try to get you to clean your plate or eat your dessert."

"I promise you, I won't get mad. But I can only eat so much, you know, to start with anyway, until I get more used to the whole food thing. But I wanna make sure that I'm eating as much as I can, and not just salad and veggies either."

"Great." Now he looks at his watch and I see that it's almost three.

"We should probably go inside," I say.

He stands up and gives me a hand. "You're going to beat this, Emily."

"Really?" I look up at him with hopeful eyes. "You really think so?"

"I do. But I agree with Leah, you *do* need help." He holds the door open for me. "I mean, I can tell you're a strong person, but you can't do it alone. First off, you need to lean on God. Remember what 2 Corinthians 12:9 says—that God's strength is made perfect in our weakness. But you can lean on me too."

"Thanks," I tell him as we go inside. And, really, I feel as if a huge weight has just been lifted off me. Oh, I'm not light and free and ready to fly. But I think maybe I can function.

It surprises me that I feel more able to focus this afternoon as we rehearse some songs. I have a feeling it's from eating the banana and drinking the juice. Amazing how food can affect your performance. Kind of like putting fuel in your car, it just runs better. I guess God knew what he was doing when he designed us like this.

"You have a really great voice, Emily," Harris tells me as we're wrapping up. "How would you feel about doing a solo sometime? Like maybe during campfire? I have this song I'd like us to do, but I think you would totally rock in the vocals. You game?"

"I, uh, I guess so. I mean, I could at least try it at rehearsal. Then if you think I can swing it, well, I'll give it my best shot."

"Cool. I'll give you the music after dinner. That way you can look it over and we can start working on it tomorrow."

"What song is it?" I ask, thinking perhaps I already know it.

"It's one that I wrote."

"Oh." I nod. "Very cool."

He shrugs. "We'll see, huh?"

So then we play for dinner. And tonight, I feel a little more relaxed and find myself actually looking at the campers a bit more as I play and sing. But I have to admit, if only to myself, that I'm still not comfortable around them. I feel really sad, like why did God allow all these problems and birth defects and illnesses and stuff? But I try not to focus on this as we do our songs, since we're supposed to smile and look happy. And I suppose it's encouraging to see how much these kids appreciate the music. It really does seem to be a highlight for them. And I gotta think that's pretty cool.

Then it's time to eat again, and I tell myself to just chill—that I can do this, one bite at a time. But, as it was before, each bite is still a challenge, and I can't get rid of the nagging thought that I am putting on weight every time I swallow. It's an obsession. But finally, I think that I'm done. There's still food on my plate, but it's better than I did at lunchtime.

"Gonna eat that?" asks Brett, pointing to my untouched black-berry cobbler topped with whipped cream.

"You want it?" I offer.

He just frowns at me. "Come on, Emily," he urges me quietly. "It's really good and berries are supposed to be healthy. Try it."

So I pick up my spoon and take a spoonful, careful to get only the dark berries—not the crust or whipped cream. I hesitantly taste the berries, and to my surprise they actually do taste good. And so I eat another bite. Before long I have eaten all the berries from my cobbler, leaving the crust and cream behind.

"Not bad," I say to Brett.

"Not bad," he says back. And I notice Harris watching us as if he's curious as to what kind of game we're playing here. And that's when I remember the verse he read to us before rehearsal today. I do remember the reference was James 5:16, but I can't remember the exact words—except that it had to do with confessing your sins to each other and praying for each other and, consequently, getting healed. I couldn't believe how hard it hit home with me, although I didn't say anything at the time. The reason Harris shared this particular verse, he said, was because he wanted the worship team to get close, close enough that we could confess things and pray for each other. "It's how God is going to be glorified by our music." But after he said this we all got very quiet, and maybe even self-conscious. Then he just prayed and we started to practice. But it's like that verse has been haunting me ever since.

"I'm anorexic," I blurt out to Harris and Nick.

Brett looks slightly surprised by my admission, and *I'm* actually shocked. But Harris and Nick just look at me, and I can't read their expressions.

"But I'm trying to stop," I continue. "Maybe I'm a recovering anorexic."

"That's cool," says Harris. "Better to be recovering than stuck in it."

"Yeah," agrees Nick. "I'm a recovering alcoholic."

Well, this is pretty stunning to me, but I try not to show it. "Anyway," I say, "because of the verse you shared today, Harris, about confessing stuff . . . well, I kinda knew that it applied to me."

He smiles. "Cool. I was getting worried that maybe I'd misheard God on that one. But I got this really strong impression that I was supposed to read that verse, that it was for the welfare of the whole group."

"Well, you really nailed me on it. I mean, I'd already confessed it to Brett. He and I were prayer partners at a camp last June. We were both counselors and both had these problem kids. So I asked him to be my prayer partner with this too, since I'm still really struggling with it—kind of like a spiritual battle, you know? I hadn't really planned on telling anyone else until you hit me with that verse. So I just thought I might as well confess it to you guys, just get the ugly out into the open."

Nick laughs. "I like that—get the ugly out into the open."

"And then you find you're not the only one with problems," says Harris.

"Yeah, that's kinda comforting."

"Well, I'm really glad you told us," says Harris. "Now we can all be supportive of you." He glances at my picked-over dessert now. "Hey, you gonna finish that off or not?"

I laugh. "Hey, I think I did pretty good to just get the berries down."

"Cool," he says as he reaches his spoon across the table and scoops up my leftover whipped cream. "I'll take care of it for you then."

Nick laughs, then pats his rotund belly. "Better you than me, dude."

I just hope that I'm not going to start resembling Nick now. I mean, I may *think* I'm beating this thing, but I can tell there's still a huge part of me that's still dragging its heels. I know the battle isn't over. In fact, it's probably barely begun.

nineteen

I CALL LEAH THE NEXT DAY TO REPORT MY PROGRESS. SHE SEEMS QUIETER THAN usual, like maybe she's feeling down, so I blab on and on, filling up the dead spaces as I tell her about my life and how I actually asked Brett for prayer support, then even confessed my anorexia to the rest of the worship team. Finally I pause to take a breath.

"Good for you." Her voice sounds tired and far away, and I can tell that something's not right.

"Leah, are you okay?"

"It's Becca," she says in a serious tone. "She's in the hospital."

"What happened?"

"*She's bulimic*, Emily!" The way she announces this reveals how shocking she's finding this news. "Can you believe it?"

"Actually, I figured she was."

"*You knew?*"

"Well, I saw, or rather heard, her hurling in the bathroom one day last spring. And when she came out, she seemed perfectly fine. Happy even. I kind of figured that's what was up."

"And you didn't tell me?"

"I guess I thought you knew. I mean, isn't it kinda the norm with a lot of models who want to stay skinny? Like in Chicago," I remind her. "You'd have to have been blind and deaf not to know that a bunch of those girls were either anorexic or bulimic or both."

"I had my suspicions."

"Well, I had *actual* conversations, Leah. They even gave me tips on how to do it. That's probably when I first crossed the line—stopped eating and started overexercising, you know. I just followed their example. Although I assured myself at the time that I would never take it as far as some of them had. I mean, some of those girls were like walking skeletons. Remember that Saundra chick from Atlanta?"

"Ugh. Don't remind me. Anyway, back to Becca. She's damaged her esophagus from throwing up so much. And she probably has ulcers too. But that's not even why she was admitted."

"Why?"

"LaMar said she had a seizure while they were doing a fitting for a back-to-school fashion show. They had to call an ambulance and everything. By the time they got her to the hospital, her electrolytes were really a mess. She could've died. It didn't take long for them to find out she was bulimic. I guess her parents are totally freaking."

"That's gotta be hard. But why did LaMar call *you* about it? Not that you don't care, but it's not like you and Becca were exactly close or anything."

"Because Becca can't do the fashion show now and LaMar really wants me to take her place."

"Are you?"

"I don't know . . . I'd already told him that I'm kinda done with that now."

"So you're really finished with fashion then? Seriously?" Okay, part of me is glad, since it seems like modeling stuff was always taking Leah away from me, but part of me feels bad for her. I mean, I know how much she loved it and how good she was at it. It's just that the breast-reduction surgery sort of took her over the edge. Kind of the way anorexia took me over the edge.

"I don't know, Emily. I told LaMar that I'll pray about it, but he wants a decision by tomorrow morning. I mean, I have no doubts that obsessing over fashion and looks is totally wrong. And I know it can really mess you up. But Aunt Cassie keeps telling me—and you know she *is* a Christian—that fashion in itself isn't sinful. It's just that it can get out of control. But she also keeps saying that the industry could really use some strong Christian influence, that it might even help to bring back some balance—as well as clean it up, you know. I guess she's kinda got me thinking, and now I'm not so sure."

"You're right to pray about it, Leah," I finally say. "And I'll be praying for you too. And when you put it like that, I can actually imagine God using you in the fashion industry. But you'd have to be strong enough to speak out and not fall into the gotta-be-perfect trap again."

"As well as not lure anyone else into it either." She sighs. "I still feel kinda responsible for you, Emily. Like if I hadn't started that stupid swan project, well, maybe you wouldn't have become anorexic."

"Hey, that was my choice, Leah. You never encouraged me to diet that way. Sure, I might've been jealous of your looks, but that's not your fault. I just took things too far. I wanted results too fast. I was stupid."

"More and more, I really am seeing it's all about balance. I mean, I don't think God wants us to go around looking like crud and letting our bodies get all out of shape. But as soon as we start focusing on only the outside, it really messes with our minds and our spirits. Don't you think?"

Considering my experiences this summer, with my fuzzy think-ing and flimsy prayer life and all that, it's obvious to me now.

"I think you're right on, Leah, and I wish I could say that I was living with that kind of balance in my own life, but the truth is, I'm not. Yet. I just hope that I can find that place. Honestly, I get so scared sometimes that I won't really escape this—that I'll go back to anorexia just to keep the weight off. That's how badly I *don't* want to be fat. I want it so much that I'm worried I could actually sin to get it—and it's freaky."

"Just take it one day at time," she says in a calm voice. "Better yet, just one meal at a time."

"How about one bite at a time?"

"Yeah, whatever works for you."

"Well, at least I've got a support system here. I'm pretty sure these guys aren't going to let me get away with much."

She laughs. "That's so perfect. Three worship-leader dudes keep-ing their eyes on you. God really does work in mysterious ways."

"Yeah, it's pretty weird if you think about it."

"And he really does have our best interests at heart."

"Too bad we don't always get it."

"Well, pray for me about the fashion show, Em. And I'll keep praying for you to beat this thing."

"Thanks. And I'll be praying for you."

"I wish you were here to go visit Becca with me. I have no idea what to say to her, but I feel like I should go."

"You'll be fine, Leah. Just love her. You're good at that. And that's probably what she needs more than anything right now. I mean, I know how it feels to put your body at risk for the sake of *beauty*."

"You and me both."

After I hang up I start practicing the song that Harris wants me to sing. I can't believe how amazing the lyrics are—it's like it was written for me. It's about how we can't do anything on our own, how we are totally helpless without God, but how we sometimes think we don't need him, that we can get by, and then we fall flat on our faces. But that's when he picks us up and cleans us off. Anyway, I sing the song again and again, and by rehearsal time, I know it by heart—I mean *really by heart.*

"I love your song," I tell Harris as we start warming up.

"Cool."

"I mean, seriously, did you write it for me?"

He laughs. "I wrote it for me . . . and everyone."

"Well, it's awesome."

"So you want to do the solo?"

"I'm not sure about that. You be the judge."

And so we go through practice and finally get to that song and I sing the lyrics and when we're done, all three guys are just staring at me.

"That was incredible," says Harris finally.

"Amazing," says Nick, and he actually wipes a tear from the corner of his eye.

Brett just shakes his head. "I'm speechless."

"Wanna do it tonight?" asks Harris. "For campfire?"

"Do you think we're ready?"

"Might as well give it a shot," says Harris.

"And I'm guessing that if it's a hit, and it probably will be," adds Nick, "the kids will want to hear it again and again."

So we do the song at the end of campfire following Harris' testimony, which is really amazing. I never would've guessed that Harris' dad was a drug addict and his mom an alcoholic. I mean, this guy seems so solid, so grounded. But, as he tells everyone, it wasn't always like that. He's had way more than his fair share of struggles. My trials pale in comparison.

Everyone seems really touched by his song, and when Pastor Ray gets up and gives an invitation for people to dedicate, or rededicate, their hearts to Jesus, it seems that everyone responds. And when he leads us all in the salvation prayer, there are tears flowing freely. It's an amazing night. It's like we came and did our thing, and God showed up—in a really big way.

As I'm putting my guitar back in the case, I can sense someone standing directly behind me.

"Can I have your autograph?" asks a girl's voice.

"Huh?" I turn around to see this teen girl. I've noticed her before. Okay, I've noticed that she has no arms. But now when I look at her, I notice she has this truly great smile. I smile back and try not to stare at the empty spaces where her arms should be hanging down.

"Are you talking to *me*?" I ask, thinking maybe she really wants one of the guys. I mean, these girls tend to really glom onto the guys, especially Brett, who is, in my opinion, the cutest of the bunch, and I think these girls would agree.

She nods. "I'm talking to you. I totally love how you sing, Emily. I just wanted to get your autograph, if you don't mind."

"But why? I mean, nobody knows who I am."

"It's for when you become famous."

I laugh. "I don't have any paper—"

"My back pocket." Now she turns around to reveal a small pad and a pen in her back pocket. "I asked my counselor to put it there so I could get you to sign it tonight."

I pull out the pad and wonder how you're supposed to do this. "Okay then, what's your name?"

"Kerry." And then she spells it for me.

So I remove the cap from the pen and write, "To Kerry, the girl with the beautiful smile." And then I sign my autograph and tuck the notepad back into her pocket. "There you go, Kerry."

She turns around and gives me that great smile again. "Thanks!"

I shake my head. "Thank *you*. By the way," I add, "do you know that you have a fantastic smile?"

Amazingly, she smiles even bigger now. "Really?"

"Seriously. It's beautiful."

"Hey, thanks."

And now I notice there are a few more kids clustered around me, all with varying degrees of handicaps—rather, *challenges*, as Pastor Ray puts it. And they want to talk to me and get my autograph and are acting like I'm actually some kind of a celebrity, which strikes me as totally bizarre. But I play along, asking them their names and where they're from, and to my amazement I begin to overlook their challenges a bit. I begin to see them just as kids—kids with big challenges. And, even more than that, I begin to see how totally shallow I've been—only caring about the surface of things.

And before I go to bed tonight, I get down on my knees and beg God to forgive me for my shallowness. I confess to him that I've been so superficial that I make myself sick. I tell him I'm sorry and that I want to start seeing things, especially people, the way he sees them.

"Please, let me have eyes like you," I pray. "Let me look beyond the physical stuff and see what lies beneath."

And before I go to bed, I unwrap the slightly stale blueberry muffin that my mom sent with me, and I actually manage to eat most of it. And for the first time in a long time, I go to bed feeling *almost* happy. Or maybe it's hopeful. Whatever it is, it's a different feeling . . . one that I haven't experienced in recent months.

twenty

"I WAS SERIOUS ABOUT MY INVITATION FOR YOU TO COME HELP OUT AT THE lake," Brett says to me at breakfast the next day. "I really am short-handed. And trying to get some of the kids safely into the life vests can be a real challenge. Plus there's gotta be a counselor in every rowboat. And sometimes the kids have to wait a pretty long time if we're short on counselors."

"Hey, I'd be happy to help," I tell him as I pour what I'm guessing is whole milk onto my oatmeal. I follow this up with a spoonful of raisins and even some brown sugar, and I try not to think about how many carb calories might be involved in this little meal.

"Cool," he says as he passes me a plate of toast. "Come on down a few minutes early and I'll take you through the ropes."

As I head down to the small man-made lake in the afternoon, I think it's probably a good thing that I'll have something to keep me busy—something to keep my mind off of the nagging fear that I'll probably gain ten pounds before camp is over. *Don't think about it*, I tell myself. *Don't even go there.* Even so, it's hard. It's so hard.

Brett's instructions seem pretty simple and straightforward, and we finish up with about ten minutes to spare, so we sit down on the dock and dangle our feet in the cool water. I try not to look at the width of my thighs, flattened out on the dock. I try not to imagine how they will look a month from now.

"The main thing is to help the kids feel comfortable around the water," he's telling me. "To reassure them that they're safe. It can be kinda scary being in their shoes, you know."

"Yeah."

"Any questions?"

"Not really. Although I have to admit that I've been kinda uncomfortable around these kids. I hope I don't blow it."

"I think most people feel like that, Emily, at first anyway. But if you spend enough time with them, you start to see that they're really not that different than everyone else—like it's just a surface thing, you know?"

"Yeah, I guess." Of course it's just a surface thing. Why am I so into how people look? When did I become like this, or have I always been like this and I just never noticed until recently?

"And they like having fun, just the same as we do. It's just a little more challenging."

I'm sort of amazed at Brett's attitude about all this. Like how did he get so grounded and sensible? "I'm curious why they don't just have the campers attend the regular camps. I mean, wouldn't it be better to have the kids with special needs mixing it up with kids who don't—so that everyone can get more comfortable with all this?"

"I know what you mean, and I asked Pastor Ray about the same thing last year when I helped here for the first time. He told me that it's always an option for the special-needs kids to attend any camp, but that they've had some real problems in the past, you know, with the so-called *normal* campers not being too patient or considerate of others."

"Probably campers like Kendra. I mean, she pretty much set her sights on anyone who was the least bit different from her. Poor

Penny really got it because of her weight problem, but who knows how Kendra might've offended a special-needs kid."

"Kids can be pretty mean."

"And grown-ups too." I don't admit that I'm thinking about my dad right now and the way he made me feel like a second-class citizen for getting fat. In some ways, he's not that much different than Kendra. Oh, he might say things in a "nicer" way, but it's easy to see the meaning behind the words.

"Yeah, I guess the human race tends to be a pretty superficial lot."

So I tell him about how I've been really aware of that in myself and how I'm praying for God to change that about me. "It's like I got worse than ever this summer," I admit. "I mean, all that focus on losing weight and stuff, it's like it really messed up my mind. I hope I'm not warped for life."

He kind of laughs then picks up a pebble from the dock and tosses it into the lake where it makes circle after circle of ripples. "Yeah, I know what you mean."

I'm not entirely convinced that he does, but it seems to me that Brett's got his head on a lot straighter than most kids our age.

"And just for the record," he adds, "I think I liked you better before you lost the weight."

"Huh?"

"I mean, it's not that I don't like you now, Emily. But you have definitely changed a lot this summer."

"What do you mean?"

"You just don't seem as happy as you used to be."

"Yeah, you're right about that."

"And I always kinda admired you, the way you were so easy to talk to, like in youth group and stuff. You seemed so well-grounded, so comfortable with who you were. I was actually slightly intimidated by your confidence."

"Me?" I am totally shocked now. *Confident?*

"Yeah, and I liked your humor. I loved the way you'd say some totally off-the-wall thing and crack up the whole youth group."

"Seriously?"

"Yeah. But then I noticed you were starting to change at the last camp. You didn't really seem like yourself. You kinda faded out, you know? Like, you weren't nearly as funny as usual, but at the time I just figured it was because of the girls in your cabin. Now I think it was probably more about the anorexia thing."

"That's true."

"You have so much to offer, Emily. Your music, your singing voice, your humor . . . man, I just don't see why you had to get so obsessed over this weight thing. And I happen to agree with Harris—I'm not really into skinny chicks either."

I study him for a moment. "But what about Leah?" I remind him. "You took her to prom."

"Yeah. But to be honest, it was only because of Kyle. Kyle and I are always competing with each other, you know. And he had already asked Krista to prom, but he told me that he thought Leah was looking really hot and that he wished he'd invited her instead. Well, I took that as a personal challenge, and so I invited Leah. The problem was, while she's nice and everything, she wasn't really my type, and I don't think either of us had much fun. Pretty lame."

So what is he really saying here? Could it be possible that I'm actually his type? Of course, I'm not going to ask him something so totally stupid and embarrassing. And he already said he liked me better *before* I lost the weight. But then he was probably just talking about my personality anyway, like I was so funny and stuff. Not like he was really *into* me, like as a girlfriend or anything.

"Did I offend you?" he asks suddenly. "I mean, you got so quiet."

"No . . ." I look out over the water where the circle ripples are just starting to fade away. "I was just thinking about what you said. And the truth is, I think I liked me better before I lost the weight too. But at the same time, I feel torn. I mean, the honest truth is that I'd still rather be thin than fat."

"I don't remember your being that fat—"

"Trust me, I was. But I guess the problem was that I kinda sold out a part of myself to lose weight. I mean, by using the wrong methods. It's like becoming anorexic sort of messed with my soul. And I guess I can see how that really did change me. In some ways I don't even feel like the same person I was before. I wonder if I ever will." There's a lump in my throat now and I really, really don't want to start crying.

"Hey, the Bible says that God is changing us from glory to glory, Emily, into his image. So, I'm thinking, if you stick with his plan, you can only get better!" Then he hops to his feet and squints up the hill to where a group of kids are slowly coming our way. "And it looks like the fun's about to begin." He reaches out, takes my hand, and pulls me to my feet. "Here we go."

It's not long before I discover that I'm actually having fun. Okay, I'm working hard too. And some of the kids can be kind of difficult, especially if they're scared, but it's amazing what a smile or a hug or a joke can do to lighten things up. And we have the celebrity factor working for us, since most of these kids are pretty wowed by the fact that two members of "the band" are helping them with their boat experience.

By the time we're done, I've only fallen into the lake once, and no one even came close to drowning. So, all in all, I think I did okay. But my muscles are sore from lifting and helping kids in and out of the boats. Even so, I think it's been worth it. It's so amazing to see the thrill on their faces when they're out there, the small rowboat cutting through the water and carrying them safely across the lake. And I also understand why Brett asked me to help. It's a big job.

"Thanks for helping," he says as we hang the damp life vests on a rack in the sun to dry. "Can I expect you to come back again? Or are you gonna bail on me?"

"I'm not going to bail," I say as I give an extra-wet life vest a shake. "In fact, I'll help out until the end of camp if you want." I make a pathetic attempt to flex the muscle in my arm. "And maybe by then I'll actually have some real muscles."

"Yeah, it's a pretty strenuous workout."

Okay, this reminds me that it's also a good way to burn calories, but I try to dismiss this stupid anorexic thought.

"You know, Emily," he says as puts a stray paddle into the big wooden barrel. "What I said earlier . . . about liking you better before you lost weight . . . I meant the way you *were*, you know, like your personality and sense of humor. I wouldn't be honest if I didn't admit that you look great now. All I was trying to say is that looks aren't everything, and that I really don't think that skinny girls look all that hot. Does that make any sense? Or am I just inserting my foot in my mouth?"

"I guess that makes sense."

"But I don't think you'd look good if you lost any more weight," he adds quickly. "Seriously, you look fine."

I laugh now. "Well, I don't think that's going to be a problem."

"And I think you'd look good even if you put on a few pounds, you know?"

I give him a playful slug in the arm. "Look, maybe you should stop while you're ahead, Brett. You keep going, and you really will offend me, and who knows what I might do to get back at you."

He laughs. "Okay, that sounds like the old Emily."

The old Emily, I'm thinking later on as I take a shower. Who was that girl really? I'm vigorously scrubbing to remove the lake scum that I picked up during my little dip, shampooing my hair, which I'm pretty sure smells like dead fish. But do I really want to go back to the old Emily? I mean, a part of me does. A part of me can remember a girl who was carefree and happy, but I think it was really several years ago. And in all fairness to me, it was before I put on the extra weight and before my dad started nagging me about it.

But as I towel dry, I can remember a happy era—a time when I never really thought much about my appearance or anyone else's for that matter. I didn't study myself in the mirror, worrying about the shape of my body. I simply lived and enjoyed life. And I didn't freak about what I was wearing or whether my hair looked cool or not. I just lived my life and had a good time. And, okay, I guess I do miss that girl, and I'm afraid I'll never find her again. I'm pretty sure that she's gone for good, left behind somewhere that I can't return to, just like every other twelve-year-old girl once we start to grow up. Even so, I wish I could go back there. I wish I didn't have to grow up.

***

Life settles into a very cool routine during the next few days. To my relief and amazement, I actually become friends with a lot of the campers. And by the end of the first week, I know most of them by name. I also realize that their inner strengths, their perseverance, and especially their childlike delight in simple pleasures—all these qualities have made an indelible impression on me. Despite these kids' challenges, their handicaps, their setbacks, they are not giving up. I want to be like them.

Just two days before camp ends, I am deeply touched by something. Campfire has just come to an end, and I'm standing on the perimeter, in the darkness, just watching the others. As usual, there are some kids struggling with crutches, or limping along, or manipulating their wheelchairs. But with the help of their patient counselors, they slowly make their way over the less-than-smooth trail. I know it's not easy because I've helped some of them myself. But these kids don't give up. They just keep trekking along, doing their best, and there's very little complaining.

And as I stand there watching, it just hits me — like this humongous aha moment — what a complete fool I've been! What a total imbecile! Instead of *thanking* God for my two strong legs that are able to run and jump and climb, I whined about my "thunder thighs" and "thick" ankles. Instead of rejoicing that I have two capable arms that can lift and carry and balance my body, I complained about the flab that hung beneath them. I have been totally and unbelievably ungrateful for everything. Like a completely spoiled brat, I took my healthy body for granted. I criticized it and despised it. With crystal clarity, I know that I do *not* deserve the good health that God has mysteriously blessed me with. Not only have I been unappreciative of my body and all its amazing working parts, I tortured it by over-exercising, and I put my entire health at serious risk by starving myself. What on earth was wrong with me? As I watch these kids with their less-than-perfect bodies, I feel so thoroughly ashamed of myself. I mean, how could I have been so stupid and shallow and self-centered?

"Hey, Emily," calls a voice from behind.

I turn to see Pastor Ray coming over to the sidelines to join me. I'm thankful for the darkness, because I'm pretty sure that tears are about to fall. "What's up?" I ask in a rather gruff voice.

"You okay?" he says when he gets closer.

I consider just brushing this moment off, but then I realize that it's too big to ignore. "I was just thinking about something," I begin sort of cautiously. "Like how I've taken my health for granted, but then I realize how others have it really hard, you know? I guess I was feeling pretty guilty. Kind of convicted, you know. Like I have so much and then I start whining about stupid things and . . . and . . ." Okay, now I really am crying.

He puts an arm around my shoulder and gives me a gentle squeeze. "Hey, I think we all feel like that sometimes, Emily. Don't be too hard on yourself."

Well, I'm not so sure that he completely gets what I'm saying, but I don't want to waste his time by unloading everything on him at the moment.

"The reason I wanted to talk to you was to ask a favor," he says now.

"Sure, what?"

"Well, tomorrow's the last day of camp, and I always really pray about who gives their testimony, especially on that night, and God is always faithful to show me the right person. And guess what?"

Okay, I am fully aware that I haven't given a testimony yet. But then not all the counselors have. I mean, there is only so much time, and this camp has a lot of counselors. "What?" I ask, fearing the worst.

"God showed me that it's going to be you, Emily."

"Me?" I say in a voice that sounds like a sick mouse.

"Yep." Then he pats me on the back. "And you'll be great." Then without giving me a chance to protest or decline or simply run, he jogs on ahead to help a boy who's having difficulty getting his wheelchair over a bump.

I'm so shocked that I sit down on one of the log benches. I lean forward, putting my head in my hands and desperately wonder how I can get out of this.

"What's up?" asks Brett as he comes over and sits down beside me.

"Huh?"

"You okay?"

"Yeah," I say, lifting my head up. "Just in shock." And then I tell him about Pastor Ray's "favor."

Brett laughs. "Can't argue with God, Emily. If he told Pastor Ray that you need to share your testimony, you better do it."

"Yeah, right."

He pats me on the back now. "Hey, you'll be great. And if it makes you feel any better, I'll be praying for you."

"Thanks a lot."

He laughs again. "I can't wait for campfire tomorrow."

"Yeah, right. Me too," I toss back with sarcasm.

So for the next twenty hours or so, I am a complete basket case. Oh, I've prayed. First I asked God to get me out of this, but then I realized that's probably not right. So then I asked him to give me something totally cool to say. I even attempted to write some things down. The trash basket in my room is overflowing with all my brilliant ideas. So far, I've come up with nada, and I'm pretty sure I'm going to make a total fool of myself.

It's hard to focus on the music at campfire, but somehow I manage to get through my parts. And once again, we perform Harris' song and I do the solo. And, as usual, the kids really love it. Then we sit down with the kids and watch as some of the counselors do what I'm sure is a really funny skit, although I can't even watch it—all I can do is pray that God will do something! Like give me something to say or maybe even zap me off the face of the planet. Or maybe an asteroid could fall nearby, distracting everyone while I make a fast escape. Or how about a forest fire? I've heard that the fire danger is high right now. But finally the skit is done, and we do a couple more songs, and then it's time for me to stand up and say something. I barely hear Pastor Ray's introduction, but I sense him looking at me now, and Brett, who's sitting beside me, gives me a strong nudge with his elbow.

I stand up and go over to where Pastor Ray is waiting for me. He gives me a big grin and a pat on the back and I realize it's up to me to say something. I shoot up one more help-me-God prayer, and then I begin.

"I'm supposed to give my testimony tonight, but I've been think-ing that it's not really that interesting." I pause, and some faces look a little confused. "Okay, I'll tell you this much: I accepted Jesus into my heart about five years ago. And it was totally cool and I'm really glad that I did it, but what I want to tell you about is what's been happen-ing with me lately." And then I confess to them about how I allowed myself to become anorexic this summer, going into the details of how I starved myself and really pushed the limits. I told them how I didn't think my body—the body that God blessed me with—was good enough. "And that drove this wedge between God and me," I admit. "And because of that, I started falling away from him. And I quit pray-ing as much, and consequently I made myself completely miserable." There are tears coming down my cheeks as I continue. And I don't hold much back. In fact, I make myself sound so horrible that I feel certain these kids are going to hate me by the time I'm done.

"I can't believe how self-centered and stupid I've been this past summer," I tell them, wiping my nose on the sleeve of my sweatshirt. "And you guys are the ones who really opened my eyes these past couple of weeks. I've been watching you and seeing what a great attitude you have toward life and your own challenges and situations. You guys are really my heroes," I blurt out, "and if I could be just a little bit like you, I would be so happy. I can tell that you guys are really trusting God with your lives, and I can see that you want to live the kind of lives that will honor God and give him glory, and that's what I want too. I am challenged by you campers, and I've learned so much from you, and I'm so thankful that you were all here to help me see this. I don't even know how to thank you for all that you've taught me." I glance at the other counselors now. "And I think all you campers deserve a great big applause." And then I start clapping, as do the other counselors, and then they stand up and we all give these campers a great big standing ovation. Then I go and sit down.

After that, Pastor Ray comes up and starts to give his message, almost echoing the very things that I've said—so much so that it feels like maybe God really did show Pastor Ray that I was supposed to share tonight. And when it's all done, I really think it was the best campfire ever. Then we get up and lead the kids in a couple more songs, and as I'm playing and singing, I'm thinking this is the closest thing to heaven that I have ever experienced. And I can't believe how happy I feel. It's like I'm going to burst from it. How do you contain that kind of joy?

twenty-one

MY CAMP "HIGH" LASTED ALMOST A WEEK AFTER I GOT HOME. NOT TO SAY THAT I've been depressed since then. It's more like I just came back down to earth. But, even so, I still feel happier than I've felt all summer. And I feel that a little bit of the old Emily is back now—like I might survive myself after all.

To my surprise I only gained one pound at camp, and none since I got home, although I no longer weigh myself daily. I don't quite understand why I'm not starting to put all my old weight back on, since I've been eating pretty much like a normal person for three weeks now, but Leah keeps telling me it's because I'm getting regular exercise and, she says, "As long as you stick with it and keep eating healthy—which means no going back to your old junk-food ways—you might actually keep the weight off." Still, I'm not so sure. I mostly try not to dwell on it. And when I do start freaking out, I just use that as a reminder to read my Bible and pray. I've been doing both of those things a lot lately.

"Still, it's hard," I admit to her. "And sometimes I get scared that I could fall back into it." It's Labor Day, and school starts tomorrow, and somehow Leah talked me into going with her to visit Becca today. And just thinking about Becca and her struggle with bulimia reminds me of how easily I got pulled into that bizarre lifestyle only a few months ago.

"Just say no to anorexia," she says as she stops at the red light.

"That's what I'm trying to do," I assure her, "but it's still a daily thing. And I still get tempted to skip meals sometimes, like yesterday when my favorite pair of jeans felt a little tight. And I have to avoid mirrors when I'm obsessing over my weight."

"Well, anorexia and bulimia are addictive behaviors," she says as she parks her car on the street in front of the clinic. "Becca said that she couldn't kick the habit without an actual intervention."

Leah already told me about how Becca's family and friends confronted her while she was still in the hospital, encouraging her to get specific treatment for her eating disorder. I guess I was a little surprised that she actually agreed to it. "And so she's really okay with it? Being in treatment, I mean?"

"I don't know for sure. I mean she kind of waffles around. Like sometimes she says how she never wants to go back to that, and then she totally flip-flops and acts like it's no big deal, and that she can keep on bingeing and throwing up and everything will be just fine. Did I tell you that her teeth are messed up?"

"Yeah. That's so sad."

"I'm so glad you agreed to come with me today, Emily." We're out of the car now, walking toward the building. "Maybe you can tell her how you got over it."

And so we sit in Becca's room and I do my best to tell her about what happened to me at camp and about the special-needs kids and how their acceptance of hard challenges really got to me. Finally I tell her how I could never have gotten better without God's help and how even now I have to pray and read the Bible just to get through it sometimes. And, although she listens, I'm not sure she really gets it.

"So have you gained any weight since you quit?" she asks.

"Yeah," I admit. "But only about a pound, I think."

She frowns. "So far . . ."

I cringe inside, knowing she's right, and I haven't weighed for several days, and it's possible that I've put on more, and suddenly I feel like I'm obsessing again. So I shoot up a silent prayer, asking God for his strength to replace my weakness.

"Look, Becca," I finally say. "All I know is that I'm thankful that God gave me the body that he did. And that it's wrong to treat my body the way I'd been doing. Putting your health at serious risk just to lose weight isn't just stupid, it's sinful. It's like slapping God in the face. And I don't want to live like that. Never again."

She kind of nods without looking up. "Yeah, Emily, I know you're right, but I'm just not there yet. You know what I mean?"

I reach over and put my hand on her arm—her very thin arm. "I understand, Becca. And that's why you're getting treatment. And I think that, in time, you're going to get past this. And both Leah and I are going to be praying for you. Because I really believe you're going to need God's help to kick this."

We stay and talk to Becca for about an hour, and sometimes it seems like she's really getting it, but then, as Leah already said, Becca seems to be waffling a lot too. By the time we leave the clinic, I'm not really sure whether our visit was helpful. At least not to her anyway.

But after I get home and really think about it, I decide that this afternoon was helpful to me. Just seeing Becca being so flaky and so unsure about everything, seeing how she's so freaked about putting on weight and, most of all, seeing how she's so completely unhappy about her life in general . . . well, it just really drove this thing home for me. And with God's help, I think I am done with it for good.

Just the same, I've decided that I might need some professional help too. And for that reason, I called up an eating-disorder clinic to get more information about the support group that meets there on Thursday nights. And I signed myself up. My first meeting is scheduled during the first week of school.

Mom not only understands why I need to go but she's also really supportive, not to mention greatly relieved. Of course, my dad doesn't quite get it.

"An eating disorder?" he says after I tell him that I'm going to the meeting tonight.

Bracing myself, I briefly tell him about my recent battle with anorexia.

"Anorexia?" he repeats, a confused expression on his face, almost as if he doesn't believe me. "I thought you were just dieting, Emily."

"It was a pretty *extreme* diet," I tell him.

"But at least you lost the weight," he says with a victorious smile, like all that matters is looking good—no matter the cost.

I look hopefully at Mom. "Maybe you can explain this whole thing to him."

She nods with a sad expression. "Yes. You go along to your meeting and I'll try to help him understand."

Poor Mom, I think as I drive to the treatment center. But maybe this will be good for her. I have noticed how she's been trying to eat more sensibly since I got home from camp. Lots more fresh fruits and vegetables around, and no more sneaking Krispy Kreme donuts into the house, at least none that I've seen. Even so, I think she and Dad need to talk about some of this stuff, get it out into the open and face it head-on.

Not that I blame my parents for the stupid choices I made. Oh,

I realize they played a part in this, but when it came right down to it, I was the one who totally blew it. I thought I was getting control of my life, but I was actually spinning out of control. And, on the same token, I'm the only one who can fix my life now—and keep it fixed. Well, with the help of God, that is. I'm fully aware that I can't do this alone. Thank God I don't have to!

reader's guide

1. Which character do you most relate to? Why?

2. Emily grew desperate to change her appearance. Have you ever felt desperate to change something about yourself? What?

3. What do you think caused Emily's distorted body image? Why did she still see "thunder thighs" after she lost weight?

4. How did you feel when Leah decided to get breast-reduction surgery? What advice would you have given her?

5. Leah was highly influenced by the fashion industry. Do you think our American culture is partially to blame for the way women perceive themselves? Explain.

6. How much influence did Emily's parents have on her in regard to her weight and eating disorder? What could they have done differently? How could Emily have asked for these things (if at all)?

7. Why do you think that Emily's bout with anorexia built a wall between her and God?

8. How do you think God wants you to treat your body?

9. Do you think you spend more time focused on your exterior person (looks, weight, . . .) or on your interior person (heart, soul, mind, . . .)? How can you stay balanced?

10. Emily finally reached the place where she was thankful for the way God designed her. Have you come to that place yet? Why or why not? What would it take to get you there?

Resources for more help and information on eating disorders

National Eating Disorders Association
603 Stewart St., Suite 803, Seattle, WA 98101
Business Office: (206) 382-3587
Toll-free Information and Referral Helpline: (800) 931-2237
http://www.nationaleatingdisorders.org

Christian Answers Network
PO Box 200
Gilbert, AZ 85299

http://www.christiananswers.net/q-eden/eatingdisorders.html

http://kidshealth.org/teen/food_fitness/problems/eat_disorder.html

TrueColors Book 10

Bright Purple

Coming in September 2006

The story of a girl who has to tackle the tough questions about homosexuality without losing her friends in the process.

One

MY BEST FRIEND JUST TOLD ME SHE'S A LESBIAN. *A LESBIAN*!

Just like that, as we're sitting in the food court at Greenville Mall, Sam calmly makes this little announcement, then adds, "I just thought you should know."

"Real funny." I roll my eyes at her and attempt to turn my attention back to my half-eaten veggie burrito. Sam and I have been best friends since grade school, and she's always had this really offbeat sense of humor. "Give me a break," I tell her. "Can't you see I'm trying to eat here?"

"I'm serious, Ramie."

"Yeah, right." But even as I try to brush her words away, my head begins to feel a little fuzzy and my upper lip actually starts feeling numb. And somewhere, deep down in the pit of my stomach, I think maybe she really is serious.

"I decided to come out of the closet," she continues. "And I need you to believe me, Ramie. Trust me, it's not like it's easy to say this to you."

I force myself to look at her now. Her expression is dead serious, and I don't think she's joking. But at the same time, she doesn't really look quite like herself either. Something is different, and I'm wondering if this really is the same Samantha LeCroix that I grew up with. The girl who moved in down the street when we were in fourth grade? The girl who taught me how to play soccer and basketball? Is this really the same girl I've shared secrets and sleepovers with? Oh, sure, she has the same short, curly brown hair, those same dark, penetrating eyes, but something is different. And it's like I suddenly feel frightened of her. A shockwave of this reality shoots through me. "You really mean this," I manage to say in a raspy voice. My upper lip is so numb that it feels like it's been shot with Novocain, and I actually reach up to touch it, to see if it's still there.

She just nods, her dark brows pulling together in a deep frown.

"Sam?" I hear the strain in my voice as I stare at her, making this silent plea with my eyes, like, *tell me this isn't really happening.* Or that it's just a lame joke. Or wake me up and announce that I've been having a horrible nightmare.

She sighs, then presses her lips together as if she's afraid to say another word. And that's when I start to feel sick, like I'm going to hurl, like I better get out of here fast.

"I gotta go," I say as I make a dash to the bathroom, barely in time to lose my lunch in the toilet. I stay in the stall for a while, trying to catch my breath as I lean my back against the cool metal of the door and blankly stare at the bright purple walls that surround the toilet. I am trying to process what I've just heard. Trying to decide whether this is for real. It's possible that Sam is just pulling a fast one on me. Maybe she's trying to teach me a lesson, to get me off her back for trying to match her up with Joey Pinckney from youth group. Okay, I'll admit the kid is kind of nerdy, but at least he's a nice guy and a strong Christian too.

"You left your purse at the table," she says from the other side of the door.

"Thanks," I mutter, still unable to emerge from my temporary shelter.

"You okay, Ramie?"

"Must've been that stupid burrito," I say as I flush the chunky remains down the toilet. "Guess those beans were bad or something."

"Yeah, I've warned you about that restaurant. BJ still swears she got food poisoning from their fish tacos." Her voice sounds a little lighter now, and as a result I experience this faint flicker of hope, like maybe this really is just a hoax. Maybe it's like that *Tom Green Show* where people get scammed while the camera is running. Maybe Sam is wearing a minicamcorder right this minute.

"You were jerking me around out there, weren't you?" I say as I tear off a big strip of toilet paper and wipe my mouth, then loudly blow my nose. "You didn't really mean what you said, did you, Sam?"

No answer.

"*Sam?*" I take in a deep breath, steadying myself to go out and face her now, to convince her that this joke is in really bad taste, but I won't hold it against her—if we can simply forget the whole thing.

"I just wanted to be honest with you, Ramie. I thought it was about time I told you the truth about me."

I lean my head against the door with a dull thud then tightly shut my eyes. How can this be? How can we be sitting there, happily eating our lunch, and Sam suddenly announces that she's gay? Like who does that anyway? And how is it possible that I never even saw this coming? I mean, if your best friend can't guess that you're gay, how can you be sure that you really are? And what does that suggest about me? Does Sam think that maybe I'm gay too? That she and I can be lovers now? Ugh! Or is it possible that I actually am gay and don't even know it? And what will our friends think when they find out about this? Or our families? Or the church for that matter? And how can Sam still be a Christian if she's a lesbian?

Way too many questions race around in circles through my head until I am seriously dizzy. I feel like Dorothy in *The Wizard of Oz*, trapped inside the little farmhouse that's being spun by the tornado. Only I'm trapped in this purple metal cubicle that's whirling around and around, as my entire life spins totally out of control.

about the author

MELODY CARLSON has written more than one hundred books for all age groups, but she particularly enjoys writing for teens. Perhaps this is because her own teen years remain so vivid in her memory. After claiming to be an atheist at the ripe old age of twelve, she later surrendered her heart to Jesus and has been following him ever since. Her hope and prayer for all her readers is that each one would be touched by God in a special way through her stories. For more information, please visit Melody's website at www.melodycarlson.com.

ALSO FROM MELODY CARLSON

Dark Blue: Color Me Lonely

Brutally ditched by her best friend, Kara feels totally abandoned until she discovers that these dark blue days contain a life-changing secret.

1-57683-529-4

Deep Green: Color Me Jealous

Stuck in a twisted love triangle, Jordan feels absolutely green with envy until her former best friend, Kara, introduces her to Someone even more important than Timothy.

1-57683-530-8

Torch Red: Color Me Torn

Zoë feels like the only virgin on the planet. But now that she's dating Justin Clark, it seems like that's about to change. Luckily, Zoë's friend Nate is there to try to save her from the biggest mistake of her life.

1-57683-531-6

Pitch Black: Color Me Lost

Morgan Bergstrom thinks her life is as bad as it can get, but it's about to get a whole lot worse. Her close friend Jason Harding has just killed himself, and no one knows why. As she struggles with her grief, Morgan must make her life's ultimate decision — before it's too late.

1-57683-532-4

Look for the TRUECOLORS series at a Christian bookstore near you or order online at www.navpress.com.

truecolors

THINK

Burnt Orange: Color Me Wasted

Amber Conrad has a problem: Her youth group friends Simi and Lisa won't get off her case about the drinking parties she's been going to. *Everyone does it. What's the big deal?* Will she be honest with herself and her friends before things really get out of control?

1-57683-533-2

Fool's Gold: Color Me Consumed

On furlough from Papua New Guinea, Hannah Johnson spends some time with her Prada-wearing cousin Vanessa. Hannah feels like an alien around her host—everything Vanessa has is so nice. Hannah knows that stuff's not supposed to matter, but why does she feel a twinge of jealousy deep down inside?

1-57683-534-0

Blade Silver: Color Me Scarred

As Ruth Wallace attempts to stop cutting, her family life deteriorates further to the point that she isn't sure she'll ever be able to stop. Ruth needs help, but will she get it before this habit threatens her life?

1-57683-335-9

Bitter Rose: Color Me Crushed

Maggie's parents suddenly split up after twenty-five years of marriage. The whole situation has Maggie feeling hurt, distraught, and most of all, violently bitter. She's near desperate for someone who can restore her confidence in love.

1-57683-536-7

truecolors

THINK

Burnt Orange: Color Me Wasted

Amber Conrad has a problem: Her youth group friends Simi and Lisa won't get off her case about the drinking parties she's been going to. *Everyone does it. What's the big deal?* Will she be honest with herself and her friends before things really get out of control?

1-57683-533-2

Fool's Gold: Color Me Consumed

On furlough from Papua New Guinea, Hannah Johnson spends some time with her Prada-wearing cousin Vanessa. Hannah feels like an alien around her host—everything Vanessa has is so nice. Hannah knows that stuff's not supposed to matter, but why does she feel a twinge of jealousy deep down inside?

1-57683-534-0

Blade Silver: Color Me Scarred

As Ruth Wallace attempts to stop cutting, her family life deteriorates further to the point that she isn't sure she'll ever be able to stop. Ruth needs help, but will she get it before this habit threatens her life?

1-57683-335-9

Bitter Rose: Color Me Crushed

Maggie's parents suddenly split up after twenty-five years of marriage. The whole situation has Maggie feeling hurt, distraught, and most of all, violently bitter. She's near desperate for someone who can restore her confidence in love.

1-57683-536-7

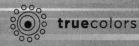